Rustam Mirsaidov was born in 1999 in the Central Asian country called Tajikistan. He was raised in his hometown, Khujand City. Reading plenty of novels inspired him to become an author and start writing his own books. Currently, he resides in Dubai, United Arab Emirates.

The book is not dedicated to anyone. Various life events and books inspired me to write my own books.

Rustam Mirsaidov

DALER: A NOVEL

AUSTIN MACAULEY PUBLISHERS™

LONDON • CAMBRIDGE • NEW YORK • SHARJAH

Ordering Information
Quantity sales: Special discounts are available on quantity purchases by corporations, associations, and others. For details, contact the publisher at the address below.

Publisher's Cataloging-in-Publication data
Mirsaidov, Rustam
Daler: A Novel

ISBN 9798891554078 (Paperback)
ISBN 9798891554092 (ePub e-book)
ISBN 9798891554085 (Audiobook)

Library of Congress Control Number: 2024901445

www.austinmacauley.com/us

First Published 2024
Austin Macauley Publishers LLC
40 Wall Street, 33rd Floor, Suite 3302
New York, NY 10005
USA

mail-usa@austinmacauley.com
+1 (646) 5125767

I want to thank my family members and people who are close to me for always supporting me. And I would like to thank Austin Macauley Publishers for their great work in publishing my book globally.

Table of Contents

View   11

Dubai   18

Arrival   29

Summer   44

China   60

Friday   79

Weeks   96

Semester   105

Nature   124

Sounds of the Waves   131

View

"What was your country again?" she asked me.

"Ahh, Rebecca, even though we've known each other for such a long time, you still cannot remember my country's name," I sighed.

"Sorry, well, I do remember where it is located though. Central Asia!"

"Yes, that's right. But think well, try to recall our conversations. I will ask you again at the end of the day." We sipped our coffee with a beautiful Marina Bay **view** from our tall building's window. We finished our breakfast and proceeded to dress up. It was a hot summer, middle of July. It is usually the hottest time in the U.A.E. She wore her pink crop-top with white shorts and Fila shoes. I wore a simple plain blue t-shirt with my light-gray shorts and Nike Air Max 90.

We left the building. I decided to take her to Dubai Mall and see Burj Khalifa on her first day in Dubai. We were waiting for the cab. She complained and said.

"Pfff, so hot, I am all sweating already."

"I know, I am sweating myself. But it's cooled all over indoors here," I told her. She just looked at me and said nothing in response. The cab arrived a few minutes later.

We got in a cab. "To Dubai Mall, my friend." I gave a direction to the driver. He looked at me from the rear-view mirror and nodded. "Wow, is it always that hot here?" She asked me. "Well, you have arrived here right on the spot. But as you know, we had to use our moment and this kind of rare opportunity," I explained her. "I know. It's just… I have never felt such hotness in my life. You go outdoors and feel like melting," she sighed. "I feel you, Rebecca. Take a look at these beautiful buildings and the way metro is built." I pointed to her to the side's window. We were on the Sheikh Zayed road at that moment. There was the metro's way on our left side with wonderfully designed tall buildings. She nodded and started observing those buildings. It would be more interesting to take the metro with her, but it would be a bit tiring. First, it would take us about 25–30 minutes to reach. Secondly, there is a long way from the Dubai Mall station to Dubai Mall itself. You have to walk around 2 kilometers on metro's linked bridge to the mall. And from my own experience, I know that it is exhausting. Besides, it was her first day, and I did not want her to feel exhausted already.

We hadn't talked that much until we almost arrived at Dubai Mall. The tallest building in the world hit our sight with its beauty, and Rebecca was looking at it. The cab dropped us off at the main entrance; it charged 50 dirhams for the fare. I paid the amount, and we got off the cab. We quickly walked into the mall. The interior's cool temperature gave us some chill. "See, I told you that it's cool indoors," I reminded her. "Yeah, it's really good," she said in response. The mall was huge; we were standing for a moment, and she was looking around. I checked my watch for the time; it was 11:48 A.M. Since I knew Dubai Mall very well, I made quick plans in my head.

"Alright, Rebecca, here is the plan. First, I will give you a tour of an awesome Aquarium and its small Underwater Zoo. Then we will eat something from the food court, get the ticket to get inside of Burj Khalifa, and then we will see dancing fountains, which are outdoors of the mall. Afterward, we'll eat our dinner and go back home," I told her the detailed plans. "Sounds good to me. Looks like it's going to be an interesting day," she said gladly with a smile on her face. We reached the Aquarium. The first thing I showed her was the whole Aquarium's view without getting any tickets. If you wanted to see fishes closely, you had to buy the ticket which would allow you to go through the tunnel underneath, including the Underwater Zoo, which was connected to the way of the tunnel. There were lots of different fishes swimming and different sizes of sharks, small and medium-sized ones.

"It is really wonderful," she said.

"Do you like it?"

"Yes, we do not have such aquarium in my town. In fact, I have never seen aquariums," she said with amazement. "Wait till you see the interior then," I winked at her. I saw some excitement in her eyes. Moments later, we headed to the counter's line where we would buy our tickets. There were only a few people on the line, so it took us just 10 minutes to stand there.

Our turn came. "Good day, I need 2 tickets for the Tunnel walkthrough and Underwater Zoo."

"Good day," the host greeted us. "Alright, understood. That's 200 dirhams," she stated the price. I pulled out my wallet from my shorts' side pocket and took out my dad's credit card to pay for our tickets. She tapped my card and returned it to me. "Here are your tickets. Enjoy your time."

"Thank you," I said in response, and we entered the tunnel. There were tons of different breeds of fishes swimming around the tunnel's rounded glass. The brown shark was unhurriedly swimming on our left side, close up against the tunnel's glass.

"Oh my God," she said. "So amazing, please take a photo of me beside this shark," she asked me.

"Alright," I took my phone out of my pocket, clicked the camera app. "The camera is ready," I said to her. She smiled and touched the glass while the shark was swimming. Then I quickly took a few photos.

"Everything is done, take a look," I showed her the pictures. She looked at my phone and was content with the quality of the photos.

"Thanks. Don't forget to send the photos to my WhatsApp when we reach home," she said. We spent some time at the tunnel, seeing all those beautiful fishes. Then we went down the path to the Underwater Zoo. We saw lots of various sea animals in that zoo, such as otters, small rays, baby sharks, and a big, long gator which amazed Rebecca. She took lots of pictures there as well. I don't even remember how much time we spent there. When we left, her gorgeous face was glowing from happiness. I checked the time; it was 2:30 P.M. We were getting hungry, and I decided to take her to the big food court to eat, not to any restaurant.

Doesn't sound romantic, well, I needed some amounts to pay for other activities.

When we came to the Food Court, I asked her what she preferred to eat.

"So here we are. What do you want to eat?"

"I love pizza. Let's eat some pizza," she said.

I never knew that she loved pizza. Let me tell you this. No matter how long you talk to the person online, even for 10 to 15 years, you'll never get to completely know her, unless you meet her in person. We ordered 1 large beef pizza with 2 drinks. We sat down at the table and started eating.

"Tell me, Rebecca. What else don't I know about you?"

"Hm, I have told you everything about myself when we chatted often," she said.

"Well, obviously I didn't know that you love pizza."

"I craved for pizza the moment you asked me what I wanted to eat. You know it's a girl thing. When you crave or feel for something, you want to have it without a question. So, maybe I never told you because I haven't craved that much. In fact, the last time I ate pizza." She paused for a second. "I can't even recall that. I guess I confused you, anyway…"

"It's alright. There are things that I will never understand about girls, ha ha." The taste of the pizza was good. We finished our pizza and got up.

"Where will we go?" She asked me.

"The next thing we will do is to buy tickets to go Burj Khalifa's interior and watch the whole of Dubai from above."

"That's exciting, let's go."

I asked about the availability of the tickets.

"It's all booked for today. Sorry, sir. You can book for tomorrow or any other day," the ticket seller told me sincerely.

"Oh, seriously…? I was surprised for a moment about why there were no available tickets. Then it came to my mind that it was a weekend, Friday. The moment she was trying to respond to me," I interrupted her. "It's okay. We might be back later for booking."

"Sure, come back later. Thank you for understanding, sir." All the while, Rebecca was standing a few meters behind me waiting for me.

"Rebecca, unfortunately all the tickets are booked for today. We could come back later for booking for another day." She was still silent, listening to me, then I kept on. "There are lots of shops here; let's have a walk and check on them. Then when the sun sets, we'll go to see the dancing fountains outdoors."

"Hm, anything you say, wherever you take me, I will follow you," she told me. "Sweet. Let's roll!" I said. The mall was too big; we checked some famous brand's stores, then got a bit a tired. But by the expressions on her face, I could say that she liked it.

We sat on the Fashion Avenue's sofa to take a little rest. I checked the time, 7:12 P.M. We sat there for a moment then went to outdoors to see the fountains and Burj Khalifa itself. As we exited the mall, the tallest building in the world was there with all its might, Burj Khalifa. When you look up, you feel an aura from that building, as if it is saying, "I am the king of all the skyscrapers. I am the origin and the first-ever tallest building in the world that was built ahead of its time. I am the history; none of the new buildings shall surpass me!" The show of the dancing fountains did not start yet. So, to her amazement, Rebecca asked me to take tons of photos around that area. As I was taking her photos, the show had started. I stopped instantly, and we gazed at the marvelous dancing fountains. The fountains were moving, to the right, to the left, vanishing, jumping higher than the mall, under the relaxing Arabic music. "Wow, that was something else; I loved it," she said with astonishment. Afterward, we walked towards Burj Park. We crossed the opera. We spent a little time at the park. She didn't miss a chance to take photos over there as well.

"How are you feeling right now?" I asked her.

"I am feeling well, just a bit tired."

"Shall we book the ticket for the Burj Khalifa touring?"

"Mm, I am not sure; I will let you decide," she said.

"Frankly speaking, I am tired too. We have to walk a long distance again. Besides, it didn't cross my mind to do it online, which is possible to do anytime we want. We can do it at home as well," I told her.

"Yeah, that makes sense."

"Let's head home then. We'll order our dinner when we reach home," I shared the plan.

"As you say."

I looked up; the night sky was full of clouds. It seemed that the buildings would be covered by the fog later on. I thought that we did good to postpone our tour into Burj Khalifa. We wouldn't even be able to enjoy the view from the top.

Dubai

I moved to **Dubai** in 2015 after graduating from high school. Why did my dad decide to bring me here?

Once, we had a family trip to Dubai, long ago. Everyone loved it, especially my dad. He loved the environment, the way buildings were constructed, and the overall freshness of everything. My dad is a real estate investor with numerous properties in my homeland. When he fell in love with Dubai, he decided to expand his business by investing in properties here as well.

He eventually did it. Instead of sending me to study in Europe, the U.S.A., Australia, etc., he opted to keep me close to him. He researched universities in the U.A.E. and found out that it has some of the best universities, including branches of many foreign universities. I can say that, thanks to my dad's efforts and hard work, I never had any financial problems.

That summer, I finished my second year of university courses and was on summer vacation. My dad left for my hometown to prepare documents for my other family members planning to move our whole family to Dubai. I was the eldest kid and grew up with three younger sisters.

My student life was not bad. Besides struggling a little bit in the beginning, I got used to it and completed the whole two years of subjects successfully. I dated a few Chinese girls from my university, but nothing worked out for the long term.

I used to feel lonely and isolated during my entire school years, although I was always shy. My heart trembled when I tried to talk to girls. I used social media like other kids around me. One day, while scrolling through my Facebook page, I saw a beautiful girl's profile photo on the suggestion list, with the name Ratanaporn Saetang. She had an innocent, adorable face with flattering light brown eye pupils. I hesitated to add her, doubting that she would add me back. "Whatever happens, happens," I said to myself. Then, I clicked the add button on my page. I got a bit nervous. Afterwards, without realizing it, I was lost in thought. Days passed, and I kept checking my friend request to her, but nothing came out of it. I felt lonely deep in my heart—a lonely teenage boy. Despite having many friends, my heart always yearned for the warmth and deep love of a girl that I could reciprocate from the depths of my heart.

It was in the cold winter of February 2013 that she finally accepted my friend request. I even remember the date, February 3rd. I recall that day in detail. It happened after 10 days of my winter school break. I was going home after my first classes of that day were over. My school wasn't far from my home, usually taking me about 10–15 minutes to reach. I had two classmates who lived near my place, so I usually walked home with their company. Besides being classmates, they were good friends of mine. We often went to a gaming area nearby to play team games, mostly on weekends. That day, I was walking with them, Jamshed and Umed. The clouds were gray, the sun wasn't visible at all, and the streets were covered with snow.

"Guys," Jamshed said. He was the most talkative one, used to bring the news that nobody knew around. Umed and I were always the first to know about something new in our class, thanks to him. I honestly never asked him how he got all the information ahead of everyone. He then continued.

"Have you heard that Negina lost her innocence to some college guy?" We were in shock when we heard it. "What, seriously?" Umed asked with surprise. "She is the quietest girl in our class. She always seemed so innocent and untouchable," I told them.

"Well, quiet people are unpredictable. They do things out of nowhere," said Jamshed.

"It is a really strange event, wow," I said to both of them. They both shrugged. "Are you guys ready for this?" asked Jamshed.

"What else could be there?" Umed responded, and we both stared at Jamshed. He then told us.

"Her mother committed suicide. When she found out about it, she could not bear it. She couldn't bear the thoughts of how other people would react to such horrible news. She was the only child. Her parents had been raising her to be a pure, disciplined girl and find a good husband for her. As you know, guys, in our culture, every future husband expects a girl to be a virgin before getting married. It's a shame for the girl to commit such an action; nobody will respect her. In conclusion, her mother could not bear all this stuff and ended her life. In addition, her father got a heart attack after her mother's death. As I heard, he is currently in a hospital."

Both Umed and I were in bigger shock from that news. At that moment, an instant thought came to my mind. "I wonder, do people in another foreign countries take this matter so seriously?" I asked myself deep inside.

"No wonder she didn't come to school today," said Umed.

"Why does nobody know at school yet? Why did nobody attend her mother's funeral?" I asked both of them.

"This is shocking news; it all happened so fast and unexpectedly that no one will have time to react yet. After all, everyone was coming out of holiday. Maybe the principal knows it and will let us know soon about her mother's death so we'd attend her funeral. Such things will take time to spread," Jamshed told us.

"Well, let it be. Whatever happens, I wish her and her family well and hope her mother is in heaven now," I said sympathetically.

"Me too."

"Me too," said both of them, repeating after each other.

I reached home, pressed the bell—ding dong, ding dong. I waited, but nobody opened. I pressed again—ding dong… I heard loud steps coming to the door. One of my sisters opened the door, the eldest one.

"Parvina, why did it take you so long to open the door?" I asked her.

"Nobody is home now; they all left to buy some fresh clothes for Dilnoza for her school, and they took Shohina with them. And I was listening to music, barely heard the ring of the doorbell." She explained to me. Shohina is one of the youngest among my sisters.

"Uh-huh, I see." I responded to her tiredly. She ran away to her room.

"What's for lunch?" I yelled, asking her.

"Mom made you some French Fries with a salad." She yelled back in response, and I heard the slam of her room's door. The loud music from her room started playing. Of course, it was one of One Direction's songs, her favorite boy band. She listened to their songs every single day. She had a dream to visit their concert one day.

I ate my lunch. The meal was delicious as usual. Then I took a hot shower, went to my room, checked the time— 2:21 P.M. I stretched my arms, sitting and yawning on my bed. She stopped playing the loud music. The whole condo was silent. I assumed she began doing her early homework. And I decided to catch forty winks. I lay down.

"It's time to get some rest," I mumbled to myself, again yawning. The moment I closed my eyes, I heard the notification sound from my phone. I checked the message; it showed from Jamshed. I opened the text.

"Daler, listen, we have been close friends in and out of school for over 7 years now. I have deep trust in you. I am sharing this news only with you, knowing you won't spread it to anyone else, and will keep it a secret between us (unless, of course, it becomes known in our entire community after some time. Or maybe it will never. God knows!). Yeah, it was a significant event for her family that her 15-year-old daughter lost her innocence so early and to some college guy. People don't commit suicide unless something is even worse than it could ever be. Here is the

thing... It's been recorded like a sex tape. Her parents found out about it, and you know the result now. The police have been searching for that unknown guy. The police report states that he was last seen days ago, before the event escalated. They couldn't find him even at his home. They questioned his parents as well; his parents were shocked to hear such news about their son. They said that their son left home for his friend's place to prepare for his big course projects. They claimed that he never lied, was always sincere with them. Therefore, they didn't question him that much. Since the police are after him, that dude is in a big trouble and won't be left without any punishments. I believe he will be found eventually, soon. I am not expecting you to reply instantly. So, take your time, and do what you were doing before receiving my text. Have a pleasant afternoon, my dear friend. Chat with you later!" Indeed, I didn't even know how to reply to that bombshell. I felt even more exhausted after reading that text.

I woke up feeling tired and hungry. I went to the kitchen to grab something. My mom was cooking pilaf for dinner and said it would be ready later, asking me to wait. I went back to my room. I checked the window; the sunset was a bit visible through the cold winter clouds. I stared for a moment, with nothing on my mind—just emptiness. I heard a voice calling my name but wasn't sure who it was; it sounded like a woman's voice. I realized that it was my mom calling me.

"Daler, the dinner is ready. Come," she called. Everyone was already in the living room, waiting for me at the table to eat dinner together. I sat down next to Parvina, and everyone proceeded to eat. My parents didn't talk to me during dinner. I guess they noticed my drained face and decided not to disturb me. I myself wasn't even feeling up to talking. I could barely eat the meal because of my exhaustion. In contrast to me, Parvina started telling about her day at school to my family, and my other sisters followed suit. My brain was so tired that I didn't even catch what exactly they were saying. My mouth was busy eating, and that was it—nothing else. I don't know why I was feeling that way on that day. I assume it's because of the heavy first day at school plus the kind of news that Jamshed informed us about. I finished my dinner last and went straight to take a hot shower. Despite the shower, I still felt fatigued. I returned to my room from the bathroom and heard the notification sound from my phone. I unplugged my phone, checked it, and the message was from Jamshed again. I wondered what else he could tell me this time. I checked the time on my phone—8:44 P.M.—and proceeded to open Jamshed's message.

"First of all, let me be polite. Good evening, my dear friend. I hope you are having a good evening. I have a news flash for you. That guy who had a sex tape with Negina… his body has been found dead under the Old Bridge. Completely dead, frozen. Police have transported his body to the hospital for investigations. Nobody knows whether it was a murder or suicide. It will be known after the doctors investigate his flesh. Look man, this world is crazy. Lots of shitty things happen. Lots of people die; some die young, some die old, some are killed—the freaking list is endless. I am myself speechless now. Was that guy a good person? Did he do that on purpose? Did he deserve to die that

young? Only God can judge that. We are mere imperfect creatures that make lots of mistakes. Some people learn from that; some try to escape. And damn, I am being here a philosopher out of nothing, for God's sake. Anyway, dude, I just wanted to share it with my best friend. I know, I know, it is negative news, and I don't like being negative myself, though, but I had to do it, share it with you first. Again, I am not expecting you to have your instant reply. You have to process it, not to mention the one earlier I have shared with you. Text me back, or we can just continue by meeting in class. I will leave that for you. I don't mind for either."

Thus, his long message was over. I decided to reply, but the moment I tried to reply him, I received a notification from my Facebook account. Since he said not to hurry with the reply, I left it for later and clicked on the Facebook app to check my notifications in detail. I was stunned. I got accepted by Ratanaporn. I had mixed feelings of happiness and excitement. That friend request acceptance from her made my day despite all the negativities I had received from school and the news. I was thinking of sending a friendly greeting text to her. My heart was pounding so fast out of anxiety to text, but despite that, I mustered up the courage and sent the greeting text.

"Hello, Ratanaporn, my name is Daler. Thank you for accepting my friend request." After that text, I switched the screen off. I was worried about whether or not I would receive a reply. A few seconds passed, and to my surprise, she replied really quickly.

"Hello, Daler, it's been my pleasure adding you as my friend. Sorry for taking such a long time to accept your

friend request. I have been busy with my classes and didn't use my Facebook much." Now, that was unexpected move from her. First of all, she replied so fast. Secondly, she explained why it took her a long time to add me back. I was astonished. I didn't know what to write in reply. It took me a few minutes to compose a response.

"I understand you. Thank you for telling me."

"Thank you for understanding me," she replied.
After that, there was a short pause between us. I texted her whatever came to my head that moment.
"By the way, where are you from?" I asked her.

"It's a bit of a long story. Do you mind if I tell you?"
"Sure, go ahead. I will gladly read about your story."
"I am from Thailand, but I was born in the U.S.A. I am currently living in Nebraska, Omaha. My dad is an Electrical Engineer from Thailand. Due to many different projects, he had to travel a lot. One of his last destinations was the United States. After all the trips, he made up his mind to reside here. My mom was always with him and followed him everywhere he went. I was born later on; thanks to being born here, I got my U.S. citizenship. My parents love my homeland, and they are very hesitant to give up their Thai citizenships in order to receive their own U.S. passports. We visit my parents' hometown, the Chiang Mai region, every year during my school's summer vacations. This is my half-long story for you."
"Wow, that's fascinating. Glad to know about you."

"*And where are you from?*" she asked me in response.

"*I am from Tajikistan, Khujand city. It's in the northern part of my country.*"

"*I am so sorry; I have never heard of such a country,*" she replied apologetically.

"*It's alright. It's a small country in Central Asia with a huge history.*"
"*Wow, happy to know where you are from. Really pleased to know you.*"

"*It's my pleasure,*" I replied. She sent me a smiling emoji after that.

"*I am sorry, I have to go now; my mom is calling me. Chat you later, alright?*"
"*No worries. Of course. Text me when you are done.*"
"*Sure.*"

Then we exchanged griming-faced with squinted eyes emojis, and our conversation was over. Despite having that short conversation time with Ratanaporn, I felt much better emotionally. My mood improved after those negative news. I chatted with her lying down on my bed. I got up from my bed, took a deep breath, sighed, and walked to the window to see the outdoors. The snowflakes were falling down, touching the ground softly, filling the whole ground with its beautiful white color. I could see the snowflakes detaily thanks to them falling down under those night lights. I looked up to see the sky. The sky was completely covered by the alluring gray clouds which were giving birth to the snowflakes.

I lost the presence. All I could see how the snowflakes were falling down from those clouds.

All of those emotions were gone. I was in a flow. Nothing came to my mind.

Moments later, the presence came back to me, and I realized that I was staring through the window, standing still. I checked the time on the clock hanging on my wall, 12:10 A.M. I felt the urge to take a pee. I went to the toilet, felt relieved after taking the pee. Returned to my room, and jumped into my bed.

Arrival

I was so excited for a few days that I couldn't even sleep out of anticipation. She bought the ticket with the flight scheduled on July 16th at 4:00 A.M., **arrival** time in Dubai. Her flight was from Bangkok. She was in her homeland with her parents for their traditional visits for every year during the summer. Close to the day of her arrival, I did absolutely nothing but count the time. With that, I couldn't take it anymore. The time hit 9:00 P.M. of July 15th, 7 hours before her arrival. I decided to go to the beach to kill some time and clear my head. I made a plan to spend there until around 12–1 A.M., then hit the road to the airport to meet her. To kill more of my time, I took the metro then a bus to get to the beach. I knew it would take me at least 1 hour.

The bus arrived at its stop. I tagged my Nol Card and got off the bus. I had to walk a little bit to the beach's way. There were lots of beautiful villas on my way. I could clearly see Burj Al Arab above all of those villas. I was thinking to myself, should I hug her when we meet? I was hesitant. I was thinking of what to say to her. What would be my first words to her in person? Should I maintain eye contact while saying my first words to her? All these thoughts gave me depression. Many different cars were roaming on two sides of the road in that area. Some of them were sports cars, some supercars, some exotic, and lots of taxis as well. My ears were covered by all those car noises. I crossed the road across to the other side. I got closer to the beach. I kept walking with all those mixed thoughts in my head.

As it was the middle of summer, the weather was hot that night, as usual. The weather has always been hot with a high level of humidity, regardless of the daytime. Since the U.A.E. has been covered with deserted lands, it was no surprise about the weather conditions out there. My pink shirt was covered with sweat. My legs were as I was wearing ripped gray jeans with white sneakers. I decided to dress a bit fashionably for our first meetup in person. I believed that first Impressions mattered a lot. In spite of the high level of heat in the weather that night, I decided to walk to the beach anyway. I could take a taxi easily, but I made my clear decision.

I had finally reached the beach site. As I was approaching closer, there was a long running line before the sand. There were also seats where people could sit at any time outdoors near the beach site. I saw a couple sitting in one of those seats. There were a Kabayan couple. In the Philippines, they call each other Kabayans, which means coming from the same country in Tagalog. I made some good Filipino friends. They taught me some Tagalog phrases. They called me Kabayan looking at my face. I was wondering why they called me that way. When I asked some of them, they explained that I look like Filipino, or at least from some Asian country. I didn't mind that, so I asked their permission to call them Kabayan too.

"So, can I call you Kabayan too?" I asked Randy, in one of our hangouts. I met him at the park one day when I was sitting alone there. We became good friends from that time.

"Sure, Daler, go ahead. In fact, you can call any person from the Philippines Kabayan. They won't even mind that; they would even be glad for that." And from that day, I could call Kabayan any person from the Philippines I could meet and talk.

"Thanks, man, gotchu." He smiled at me and showed me a thumbs up.

There was nobody around the beach site except that couple. I was wondering what they were doing out there in this kind of weather. Their faces looked tired and covered with sweat while talking to each other. "Well, love can bring you anywhere in any weather." I murmured to myself passing them by. My shoes hit the sand. I walked closely to the seashore. The water was calm and tranquil. I took a look to my left side to see the Burj Al Arab. There it was, the only hotel in the world with 7 stars, was placed there with all its beauty, with a marvelous design. I glanced down; I realized the water touched my sneakers, stepped a little back. I stared at the seashore; nothing came to my mind. My head was completely empty.

I felt the cool breeze of air coming from the seashore. The hotness was gone. "Wow, what a drastic change of the weather," I said to myself. The sweat was gone. All I could feel was the cool weather hitting my body. The feeling was amazing.

I looked around, then looked back. The seats were missing, and the couple had vanished from sight. Burj Al Arab was gone too. I didn't know how to react to that kind of situation. Darkness covered the whole place, and I could hear the waves' sound. As I narrowed my eyes to see the seashore, someone was standing there, waving at me, calling me to come closer. I could neither walk fast nor run; the way I walked was in a slow motion. At that moment, I lost all my senses, not even realizing that I was approaching her. The only thing I could do was let my sight get closer and closer to that person.

Finally, I approached the girl. She was wearing a mask on her face, and I couldn't see any other parts of her body. Her hair was long with a glowing brown color. We looked into each other's eyes. Her eyes were so ecstatic. We maintained eye contact for a moment, and she grasped my right hand, squeezed it hard. I felt warmth. Then, somebody stabbed me from my back. I lost that warmth from my hand, yet I didn't feel any pain. I turned around and saw a faceless man wearing a suit, holding a big, thick knife in his right hand, swinging and playing with it. Staring and unable to comprehend what was going on, he stabbed me again, the second stab in my stomach. I bent down on my knees from the staggering powerful stab, and my face was looking down on the sand. It took me a moment to lift my head.

I checked around, and there was nothing there. All I could see were stars in the sky; the sights of my environment were gone. The girl was gone, the faceless man was gone. I felt like I was gone myself. Was it a dream or reality? I had no idea, as I couldn't fathom anything at that time. Yet, everything felt so real.

"Hello… hellooo…? Wake up, wake up, bro…"

I heard the man's voice transcending into my ears. My shoulders were shivering from the touch.

"Are you okay...? Get up, get up." I slowly opened my eyes and saw a tall man reaching his hands to me. He grabbed both of my hands and pulled me up. I stood up, realizing I was still at the beach, near Burj Al Arab. There was nobody around the beach except for that man who helped me get up.

"Are you alright?" he asked me.

Pausing and still processing what was going on, I replied to him.

"Yeah... yeah, I am good."

"I saw you lying down on the sand. I have never seen somebody sleeping around the beach like that at this time. I usually go for a walk after the Fajr prayer every day. I got worried and decided to check you out. You are lucky that I saw you before the police did. Otherwise, they would question you." I listened to him without paying full attention.

"What time is it now?" I asked him directly, holding my head.

"It's past 4:30 A.M. now. Where do you live?"

After hearing what he said about the time, I panicked.

"Oh my God." I realized Rebecca's arrival time was 4:00 A.M. I rushed away from the man without saying a word. I started running like crazy to catch a cab to get me to the airport.

"Hey bro, hey, are you alright?" he started shouting. I didn't even look back. His voice disappeared into the distance, far, far away. While I was rushing away, I noticed tiny sand rocks falling down from my entire outfit, bit by bit. Whoever wanted to follow, it would be easy to find me from those sand prints on the way.

At last, I reached the bus stop, took a look at my watch, 4:48 A.M. There was no cab instantly, so I decided to check myself. I realized that my sneakers were filled with beach sand. I was shocked that I couldn't even feel that heaviness on my feet. I looked around; there weren't any people around, and a few cars just passed by. I took off both of my sneakers, cleared them from the sand. I made the corner where I stood a bit dirty with that sand. I did not have any other choice, I hoped that nobody saw that. While I was putting my sneakers back on my feet, I saw a cab approaching. Immediately, I waved at the cab to stop. It stopped; I got in the backseat. The driver stared at me for a second from the rear-view mirror. "Where do you want to go, sir?" he asked me.

"Ahh, Airport Terminal 1, please." He just nodded and didn't say anything. The car accelerated, passively moved forward. I checked my clothes vigilantly, wasn't able to see much dirt because it was still a little bit dark. Thank God the driver didn't notice much either. While on the way to the Airport, I took my phone out of my jeans pocket and phoned Ratanaporn on her Thai number. There were a few dial tones, still, she didn't pick up. I hung up and called again, the same thing happened. I got a little bit worried. Twenty minutes passed, and we were in the Deira area. The driver was passing by the Creek Harbour. There were lots of small and big ships moored. The sun was slowly rising on the east horizon. It was beautiful to see that day's sunrise. Out of the blue, my phone rang. I checked who was calling… It was Ratanaporn. My heart calmed down a bit, and I picked up the phone.

"Hello, Ratanaporn, are you alright? I am on my way; please wait for me."

I spoke first, my voice cracking. There was silence for a few seconds. "Hi, Daler. I got worried about you as well. I waited and waited, filled with different kinds of thoughts. My phone was on silent; I forgot to turn the volume up completely. Guess my tiredness messed up my head. What happened to you?"

"I will be there in 10–15 minutes; please do not worry. It's a long story; I will tell you when we meet."

"Alright," she said.

"I will call you as soon as I arrive at Terminal 1."

"Okay, understood. Will be waiting for your call. See you."

"See you," I said from the other line. We hung up; the call ended. The driver didn't even say a word the whole way.

The cab arrived at the Terminal 1's arrival Taxi Parking. The sun cast its light everywhere. The cab's interior became clearly visible. I was worried that the driver might notice the dirt I brought into the car. Nevertheless, I had to pay and get off the cab. The whole trip to the Airport cost me 70 dirhams. I handed him the cash from my wallet. He took the money, gave me back 30 dirhams in change.

"Thanks for the ride," I said to the driver.

"No problem," he said with a smile. Seeing his smile, I hoped that he wouldn't notice the dirt on the backseat. I got off the cab, and he observed me through the rear-view mirror. As I walked towards the entrance of the terminal, I decided to look back to see if he had noticed anything. He stared at me with a frown, then left the parking. I guessed he noticed the dirt but surprisingly didn't say anything to me, except for that stare. I assumed he had already been exhausted from his shift, and that might be the reason he didn't complain. There were lots of people from all over the world leaving and entering the terminal. I headed to the waiting seating area of the terminal, searching for her. The interior was vast, making it hard for me to find her, and there were many people sitting there. After sometime, unable to locate her, I decided to call her. I dialed her number, and in a few tones, she picked up, asking me directly.

"Daler, where are you? Have you arrived?"

"Yes, I arrived 15 minutes ago. I searched for you everywhere but couldn't find you," I told her with a tired voice. "Can you please stand up and wave at me so I could see you?"

"Okay, a moment, please."

There was silence for a few seconds. "I am standing up now. My left hand is raised. Can you see me now?" She said.

At last, I found her. She was standing with her hand raised on the last corner of the seating rows. "Oh yes," I said. I waved back at her, and she saw me too. I walked towards her direction, my heart pounding faster with excitement. I couldn't believe it was finally happening in reality after all these days, months, and years. As I approached her, I stood there looking into her eyes like a statue. She gave me a warm smile.

"Hey, Daler," she said. "I am happy to see you." I stood still; words wouldn't come out of my mouth. She came closer to me and hugged me. Her hands touched my back, and she patted me. I hugged her back, and suddenly, tears streamed down my face. As I was taller than her, my tears dropped onto her left shoulder.

"Finally, it happened. I can't believe it; you are here with me," I told her while hugging each other. When we were done hugging, I noticed that I made her outfit dirty from that situation that occurred to me earlier on.

"I am sorry; as you can see, my outfit is dirty, and I passed that dirt to your outfit." From her look, I thought that she didn't even mind that.

"It's alright, though. I am really happy to see you. As you said, you'll tell me what happened to you when we get to your place. I am sure you have a washing machine." "Definitely, I have," I responded enthusiastically with a smile on my face. She smiled back at me, and then we proceeded to leave the Terminal. I brought the baggage cart, laid her medium-sized baggage on it, and then took it to the exit. She followed me. I was still out of words as we exited the Terminal. It had gotten too hot by then, and the sun hit our heads with its heat.

"Don't worry; we'll leave immediately," I told her. I quickly caught one of the cabs at the Terminal's parking. The baggage wasn't that heavy, but I was too tired. The driver helped me to put the baggage in a taxi's trunk. To my surprise, he didn't mind our outfits' condition. We both sat in the back seat, and the interior was cool enough, so we both sighed.

"Where to?" The driver asked me.

"Dubai Marina." The driver nodded and accelerated the car from its place. And we were on our way to my place.

"So, Ratanaporn, how was your flight?"

"It was wonderful. I slept almost the whole flight."

Without me giving a response yet, she kept on. "Daler, I want to ask you something. Please call me Rebecca…"

"Oh, seriously, I have been calling you by your real name all these years. You have never asked me to call you otherwise," I told her with a surprising expression.

"Yes, I know. The matter is that nobody called me by my real name during my school years. You know, foreigners, when they heard about my name, they laughed at it and made a joke about it because of the ending of my name. I tried to explain to them the real meaning of what that word really means in the Thai language, which is 'Blessing', but they always ignored me. I came up with the name Rebecca so that the new people I met wouldn't wonder about my real name and ask too many questions or laugh. I know you always called me by my real name during our video calls, and I really appreciate that. But in person, except for my parents and relatives, nobody calls me Ratanaporn. Could you please do me a favor by calling me Rebecca for now? I need to get used to it. I am sure I will not need many days to get used to being in your presence, so you can start calling me Ratanaporn as usual."

"Wow, that is a new thing. I have never known about it until now. Alright, I will do it, Rebecca," I said, supporting her.

"Thank you for that." I nodded and gave her a smile in response. I checked on the driver; he didn't even flinch and was completely focused on the road. After that conversation, we just rested and didn't say a word until we arrived at the destination.

We reached the building address. The driver helped me carry the baggage to the entrance of the building. I thanked him, and he left us. I wanted to call security to help me get the baggage up to my apartment's floor, but he wasn't there. I guess he was patrolling around. "How did you carry this heavy baggage of yours?" I asked her.

"On my departure, my father helped me. On the arrival, I politely asked one of the Terminal's employees," she explained to me.

"Hmmm, alright. Well, we gotta carry it ourselves now." She nodded.

I held the right side, she held the left side, and we gradually pulled it to the elevator. Thank God it had two small wheels attached to its down part. I pressed the 24th floor. "Are you tired?"

"Just a little bit. What about you?"

"I feel weird now, from all the strange phenomena that occurred to me earlier on. I can't even say whether I am tired or not." The elevator hit the 24th floor, and we moved on to my apartment.

"I'll explain you in details what has happened," I told her while searching for the key in my pocket. I unlocked the door, and at last, we had reached and entered my home. The apartment was dead silent. The first thing I wanted to do was to take a good cold shower to refresh myself. I excused myself to Rebecca. "I need to take an immediate shower. Could you please wait for me in my room? I'll be done in 10 minutes." I think the fatigue hit her body as well. She nodded without saying anything. We left the baggage beside the door. She followed me to my room, where I took her. There was no window in my room, and darkness covered it. I turned on the lights. I felt a bit ashamed that I forgot to make my bed before leaving for the beach. I apologized to her for such inconvenience.

"Sorry for such a mess; I was planning to clean everything up before arrival. But as you can see from my outfit... I guess you can make an assumption about the situation."

"Ah, come on, Daler. We know each other for years. I know you very well. You don't have to apologize for anything, as if I have never seen your messy room." She said with a smile on her face.

"True," I said. Since we have made numerous video calls during our long-distance relationship, it was no surprise to her. Yet, somehow, I felt that shame. "Please make yourself at home; you can sit or lie down on my bed. I will be back in 10 minutes," I told her and left for the shower. When I finished my bath, she was still sitting in my room.

"Do you want to refresh yourself too?" I asked her. She looked as if she were lost in her thoughts, then out of the blue, she spoke. "I want to hear what happened to you. While you were in the shower, all I was thinking about was that little situation that happened to you."

"Are you sure you don't want to eat, drink...?"

"No, let me first hear that," she said with curiosity.

"Alright, but let's go to the kitchen. I want to have something to refresh my mind too. I will make tea for you as well as tell you about that situation." She nodded, and we went to the kitchen. She sat on the sofa in front of the small floor table, while I was boiling the hot water for making the tea. I didn't tell her anything until the tea was ready.

I poured jasmine tea into two mugs, laid them down on the table, sat beside her. "It's not that long, but a weird one." She looked into my eyes, showing that she was paying full attention to listen to me. I continued, "When my dad left three weeks ago, I started being excited. As you know, I have let you know about it, and we made our long-time plan come true. The day you bought the ticket, the level of my excitement rose higher. All I did was think about you, meeting you in real. That type of excitement wouldn't let me sleep at nights. Trust me, when this happens, it means that a person is so happy. I am happy. I didn't want to tell you about it, to make you worry. On the night of your arrival, just hours ago, this craziness made me go to the beach to comprehend what was going on, that I couldn't even sleep. So, I went to the beach. My plan was to spend only a few hours there, then go to the airport to meet you. The night was trivial, hot weather, hot wind blowing all over the beach. I was just standing there, listening to the waves' sound. That felt so real that I wasn't able to tell whether or not I was dreaming. I see a girl with a mask waving at me. I approach her, we look into each other's eyes, hold hands, and then boom… faceless man stabs me in my back. The girl vanishes, everything gets dark, vagueness comes… and somebody woke me up. He helped me stand up from the beach's sand. As I was struggling with what was going on, I straight asked the man about the time. After hearing the time from his mouth, I realized that I had to meet you at the airport. I rushed away from him. I think I had to at least say thank you to him. But my thoughts were only about the airport, and I couldn't help about it. As you can see, here we are."

For a few minutes, she didn't say anything in response. I didn't mind that; I let her proceed. Instead, I took our mugs from the table, handed her tea, and began sipping our tea. The hot jasmine tea slowly had got into my throat, going down to my stomach. I enjoyed the taste of the tea with pleasure. A few moments later, she broke the silence. She told me that she dated a guy during her high school time. It made feel a bit uneasy. I sort of felt a bit jealous. The fact is, she had never told me that she had ever dated somebody during our connection days. She said that she kept it a secret from everyone, even her parents didn't know about it. I listened and absorbed everything. No matter how I felt, I couldn't judge her anyway. I myself dated some girls during my semesters. So, it was fair enough. She told me that they dated for a few months only. She told me that nothing worked out between them. Besides all of that, she never felt any deep feelings for the guy. The moment she told me that, I felt a bit eased, maybe I was a little bit happy that she hadn't slept with the guy. She added more about that, said that the guy had still kept on texting her. He confessed his love to her. The last time he texted her was before her departure to Dubai. All she did was to ignore his texts because she had never had those deep feelings for him. She told me that she even blocked him from all her social media accounts. In spite of that, he found ways to connect with her. She even thought about reporting him to the police.

"I don't think it will be worth it. As long as he doesn't approach me physically, I can keep ignoring him and block him. It doesn't bother me that much."

"Some people are crazy and won't ever back down. If you receive one more text from him, I suggest you to report it to the police immediately. You shouldn't wait any longer," I told her in response.

"Hmm, maybe you are right. How long can a guy keep texting like that? It has already been 2 years since the last time I saw him. Ugh, I hope that was his last text," she sighed.

"Well, I hope for that too." We kept silent for a moment.

I would never dare to tell her about the girls that I had dated. Who knows… life is hard, circumstances fluctuate, perhaps one day it would slip out of my mouth unconsciously. After our conversation, we finished our jasmine teas. She went to take a bath as well. While she was taking the bath, I was sitting alone on the sofa, thinking, if I did right not telling her that I was no longer innocent. It was a difficult decision to keep it from her. For that time, I made up my mind it was best not to tell her and keep it to myself.

When she finished showering, we opened her luggage. Since my dad's wardrobe had been half empty that time, I decided that we place all of her clothes in my dad's room. My bed was big enough to keep two persons on it. We ordered kebabs, ate well, and then went to take a nap. On the first day, I was shy to cuddle her; we just lay down side by side. We had a good nap. After our naps, we just talked the rest of the evening. I promised her that I would take her to that beach that I ambitiously collapsed. She showed her happy emotions for that. Later on, she video-called her parents as well as me.

Summer

I waited for her text reply until the morning that night. Yet, I hadn't received anything. All the excitement that I was having was gone in a matter of a second. I thought to text her, asking her where she'd gone, but I was too unmotivated, too down for that kind of action. I checked the time, 6:20 A.M. I had only one and a half hours left to go to school. I sighed, covered my whole body under the blanket, and started crying.

"Why it is always like that? Why do I never succeed with any girl? Why?" I muttered to myself with tears on my face. My tears dropped one by one onto my pillow. I trembled. The only girl I had instant feelings for, even from a distance, left me without a reply while telling me that she would text me back later. I was so devastated. I was still in bed. Later on, my mom came to my room to check on me. She saw the condition of my face.

"I understand you are having difficulties now. By seeing your face, I can't let you go to school like that. You should take a rest. I will tell your father not to allow any of the kids to go to school today. I will blame it on the cold weather. I don't think he will make problems. Now, sleep, have a good rest. When you wake up, come to me, I will cook something for you." She petted me, kissed me on my forehead, and left my room.

I was always close to my mom. Whatever happened to me, she sensed my pain just by looking into my eyes. She never shouted at me or beat me. I was always an obedient son. Even when I misbehaved, she would pat me, kiss my cheeks or forehead, and then kindly explain to me not to behave like that anymore. Anyone would say that I was the favorite child due to that kind of treatment from my mom. However, in my opinion, parents know their kids best, and they treat them the way they think is right. For each kid, I am certain she loves my siblings as much as she loves me. My mom treated me that way because she knew my character and understood what type of parenting would work for me.

The days passed, and I returned to school in four days. I needed time to recover from that emotional damage.

Upon my return to class, I didn't see Jamshed; he was missing. I thought he took some rest as well after all those news about Negina and her family. Surprisingly, Negina wasn't in class either. The first subject of the day, Algebra, was over. The second subject was Literature, and our Class Teacher lectured us. Before the beginning of the second class, she called me.

"Daler, please come to me." I did as she told me to do. She whispered in my left ear.

"Daler, listen, you have to go to the principal's office right now. He needs to ask you a few important questions. Don't worry, you are not in trouble; just stay calm and answer his questions truthfully. Understood?"

"Yes, Mrs. Gafurova, understood."

"Good! Now go."

I had never gotten into any trouble at school. Always behaved well, showed good manners. That was the first time ever that I was called to the principal's office. I headed to his office with distress.

I knocked on the door of his office. His assistant greeted me and let me in. There he was, sitting, hands folded on the table, wearing a dark blue suit with a white shirt underneath, waiting for me. His assistant left us. I sat across his table; I couldn't look directly at his face. "Daler Sanginov, born on May 5th, 1997. 9th grader, the class of Mrs. Gafurova," he recited the information, looking straight into my eyes. "Yes, sir." I replied with my cracked voice.

"How are you today?"

"I am good, sir."

"Very well," he said, then carried on the conversation. "You might, or might not heard of it... An event has occurred recently that caused our school trouble. A big trouble! It cost us our school's reputation." He stood up, started pacing around his office with his hands behind his back. I was listening to him carefully, with fear running through my veins. He then continued. "You see, Daler, even though parents should take most of the responsibilities for their kids, the government blames schools for that. This situation is abroad as well. I see news from the U.S.A., Russia, and I can even say globally. Any sort of major negative event occurs, their governments still blame the schools. True, kids spend around 6 to 7 hours a day at school, which is a lot. It's true that kids get influenced by the teachers, by his/her classmates, from other students in other classes as well. Whatever happens at the school's location, this would be our responsibility for the student's actions. Despite that, the government blames schools for the student's actions that occur out of school. Does that sound unfair?" Before even showing any kind of response to his question, which puzzled me, of course, he kept on. "Daler! This world is unfair, not because of your own actions but because of your best friend's actions. This is real-life experience for you, to make you understand, to guide you to adulthood. This is my personal opinion. Right. Where am I going with this? Oh yes. Here is the thing, Daler. Negina Toshmatova, born on December 17th, 1997, whose age is 14 now, slept with a 22-year-old college student, whose name I have no right to bring up. The first criminal case. Second case, the tape has been recorded, uploaded to the internet, also shared from people to people. One of the worst things is this, the tape's headline was our school's name. In addition, the person who recorded their tape chants our school's name during the recording. On top of all of that, after police investigations, they found out that the person who recorded the tape was your classmate Jamshed. We found it out just 2 days ago, while you were absent. As you can see, both Jamshed and Negina have been missing from the class today. When I questioned your class teacher and your classmates, they informed me that you and Jamshed have been close friends for years. We contacted his parents, questioned them as well. But we wanted to know him personally from your side too." He stopped pacing, returned to his seat facing me again. I literally was out of any words. Jamshed, my best friend, did it. I couldn't believe that he was the one that recorded that tape. It made sense to me why he knew about that news in detail. The principal spoke up.

"Here are my questions for you. Tell me what you can about his character, about his behavior. Any odd actions? Just anything you know about him."

I had no choice but to tell him everything I knew about Jamshed. If I didn't tell, I would be in trouble myself. No matter how close friends we had been, that was the defining moment between our friendship. Deep down, I felt awful that because of another person's actions, no matter who that person was, I was there, innocent, being questioned by the principal just for none of my deeds. That moment, I truly tasted the unfairness of our lives. The principal taught me a hard lesson that day. I gulped, then revealed.

"As you say, Principal Sattorov."

"Please don't be afraid. I assure you, nothing bad will happen to you," he said, somehow calming my nerves.

My nervousness was a bit gone. "Most of our time, we played video games together. We were always a team, defeating other teams in different games. He always seemed like a wise person, knowing all the information before everyone did. He shared his secrets with me. Like how he talked to different girls, about trying to drink alcohol, and so on. Since he has been my close friend, it all seemed normal to me, sharing our moments, keeping our secrets together. I swear I have never tried alcohol. I have never slept with any girl…" He interrupted me.

"I believe you. You were always an excellent, well-behaved student. Our school should be proud of students like you. Now go on, please."

"To tell you the truth, anytime I asked him where he received that kind of information, such as Negina's incident, he always kept silence or changed the topic. It didn't bring me any harm; I didn't mind all that stuff. Never took them seriously. I always thought that it is so cool to have each other's back in close friendships; it is what defines close friendship. I had these kinds of thoughts. Never have I expected that I would be in such an inconvenient situation." He sighed, "Ah, you kids need to learn many lessons, or life will punish you before you even learn them. You are lucky that you are here now, hopefully, having learned your lesson."

"Yes, sir, I will note this for my lifetime!"

"Well done, Daler! For you to know it, both Jamshed and Negina are expected to be expelled from our school. We will go to court to determine this situation, Mrs. Gafurova and I. I brought you to my office today because I don't want your family to be in court. I will do my best so that you and your parents won't participate there. I will call your parents later to inform them about this situation. You should go now. Remember this lesson, Daler." After that, he called his assistant, and she guided me to the exit where I went straight to my class.

I blushed, felt horrible. My mind was blurred; I didn't even want to be in a class. The moment I entered my class, everything looked ordinary, as if nothing happened. Or was I tripping? I can't recall the precise memory of that moment.

That day's midnight, I had received a long confessing text from Jamshed. I was hesitating to read it as a result of that day's horrible event that occurred to me. As angry as I was with Jamshed, I decided to give it a try.

"Daler! My dearest, closest friend. You have always been like a brother to me that I never had in my family. You

have always been like family to me. I know you must have had a long, depressing, awful day today. I am sorry for that. It is my responsibility; I take it. But you already have met with the principal and revealed everything about me. I have never told you how I knew all the things that were happening in our hometown. I have been having this dark side of life since I was 12. You shared with me all of your secrets, but I didn't. I am sorry for that. Life is not perfect; some things are not meant to be revealed. Never! But you had that incident today because of me, I believe it is worth it after all. I will risk my life for that. This is my last text to you. This is for our friendship. For our long-time brotherhood.

"Adults underestimate kids' abilities. Adults underestimate kids' wit. I am the example of the underestimation. Back in the summer, 2 years ago, I was playing at the gaming center. I met one guy who was playing there as well. We got along well that day. He offered to me to hang out with him at his place. Out of my emotions, I agreed. We went to his place, we had drinks, and he even called hookers. That day's evening, I lost my virginity. I was feeling like a real grown-up man after the intercourse with that hooker. The guy was from a wealthy family. He took me to one of his dad's apartments. He was 20 that year. Days passed, I got closer to him, I trusted him more and more, he had a big influence on me. Out of school, except you, he was close to me as well. I am sorry; I always called you my only best closest friend. But that was a lie. Consequently, as that horrible news spread out with the tape, I realized that you are my only closest friend. I am not lying about this; I trusted you the most, though, and this text is the result of

that deep trust in you. That guy taught me to smoke as well. I hung out with him every Sundays secretly not telling you. In every of our hangouts, he called his other older friends too, we drank, we had sex and all those adult things that grown-ups do. I even shot up heroin. Can you believe that? I honestly don't know how his friends brought up drugs. Once I asked him, but he told me that it wasn't my business to know about that, for my own sake better not to know. I shut it, never asked about it again, and just kept on shooting myself up. I wonder how my body reacted well to those shots. At those times, I always thought it was so cool. He had lots of friends around the town. He always knew all the major news in our town. Every time something had occurred in the town, his big circle told him, then he spread it to me, then I spread it to you, but I always asked you to keep it a secret. He called this type of spread 'A word of mouth.' I am sorry again. I had a crush on her. Negina had dated me for one year. During these months, I had built her trust in me. Recently, on that day's Sunday. I invited her to Behzod's place, she accepted my invitation. I convinced her to have a drink with us. Behzod didn't invite his other friends. We were three that day. We had drinks. Frankly speaking, my memories are blurred about the details, but I know one thing, we shot up drugs as well... As you can see, that tape was released, that horrible news was spread to our school, and now everywhere around the town, maybe soon around the country. I swear to God, I don't remember any of my actions that evening's moment. I assume Behzod was aware of what he was doing, wasn't that drunk. He took advantage of us, then committed that act. You know what I am talking about. I can say now, he had been a really bad influence for me. I feel horrible right now. But irretrievable things happened now. Nobody can do anything now. I blame myself that such a thing occurred to Negina. It is totally my fault. Because of me, she lost her mother. Oh my God... What have I done...? Behzod realized that he will be put in jail for the long term, perhaps even for the lifetime. Then he decided to commit suicide. Yet, his family has been called for the court including mine and some staff from our school. In my literally short life, never ever have I thought that I would be in such a situation. I don't see any future for myself now. I have degraded my family; I have degraded my school, mostly, I have let you down in this painful way. I am so sorry about that. I will never ever forgive myself for that. I know you have a kind heart, even if you forgive me, I will never be able to do that from my side. That guilt will be buried deep inside of me for the rest of my life. From the bottom of my heart, I am really sorry. Whatever happens in the future, it is best for us to never meet again. I believe you want it more than I do. I wish you the best in your life. May God bless you all the time. I will always remember our good days that we spent time together. I will always remember you, my brother. Goodbye!"

I didn't even know whether or not to believe his words anymore. Maybe he committed that type of action on purpose without being drunk. Maybe he was just a lost teenager deep inside. Maybe he was manipulated. I made many endless assumptions. It made everything even worse, knowing all of his secrets that he kept from me. Eventually knowing his true nature... For the teenager to be backstabbed like that from his early age, it was just unbearable. Thank God my parents didn't talk to me that much after my school, earlier on, before receiving that text. It made me think a lot about friendships. Do even real close friendships exist? Do people always wear masks by being fake to each other? Do people backstab each other in that way or even worse than that? Was I always too naive? Is it in our human nature to deceive a lot, lie a lot, backstab…? I was so disappointed, sad… One thing was clear to me that I was determined not to trust anyone to be my closest friend. I made up my mind not to let anyone get that close to me. At that young age, I had learned some valuable things about life.

1. Unfairness
2. Trust
3. Friendship

I decided to trust only in my family members, my parents, and my dearest little sisters. However, I decided to never lose hope for friendships; maybe I could keep a small circle. Maybe I would have to learn a lot about that particular person to let him/her be close to me.

My parents had to attend the court eventually. They didn't tell me much about what had happened there. They warned me to be careful. They made a rule for all of us, the kids in the family, not to go anywhere with friends, classmates, no more hangouts with the other peers. Just go to school and return home. I was broken, devastated, so I didn't even protest against such a rule. This pattern continued until I finished 9th grade.

I literally was unwilling to hear any news about Jamshed, but one of the last days of my 9th grade, Umed came to me and spoke.

"Daler, have you heard about Jamshed and his family?" I didn't say anything to respond to him, but he paused for a second then continued. "Anyway, listen, rumors say around the school that his family had left the town out of this disgrace. As Jamshed is at his teenage years now, he didn't get much punishment; his parents had to pay an enormous amount to save his ass. Eh, he seemed to me like a good friend too. But he is gone now, we have to move forward. We should probably forget about him at all." I just kept listening but didn't say a word. With that being told to me, he looked at me, realized that I wasn't in a mood to talk, and then left my side to be back to his seat in the class. I had not heard a thing about Negina. Nobody said anything about her. It is like she vanished from this planet at all. The rest of the months I spent shallowly. I asked my parents not to even celebrate my birthday, not call any guests on May 5th. Nothing even interested me. I went home, ate my meals, listened to sad songs, watched some movies, didn't bother to do my homework as much as I used to. My marks decreased to an average. I didn't even want to go to school at some point. But somehow, I managed to pass my final exams. My mom did her best to motivate me as much as she could. Thus, the 9th grade was over.

The **summer** arrived; it was beginning of June when my 3-month vacation began.

As usual, I spent most of my summer vacation time at my grandparents' house. Their house was big enough for our family as well as two of my aunts and their kids. I was the second eldest grandkid from my mom's side. The eldest one was a girl named Mehrangez. The rest of my cousins were younger than me. It was always fun; we played outdoors with the neighbors' kids. The most favorite was hide and seek. We played that game after the sunset. It sounds cute and all, but the older I got, the more time I stayed indoors. I spent my time scrolling on my social media accounts, watching different movies. I withdrew myself from the world, especially that summer of 2013 as a result of all those events that had happened to me.

One day in the night of July, I received a message notification. I was too fussy to check that as I was just lying on the sofa alone, separated from the rest of my family at my grandparent's house. My eyes gazed at the ceiling; I could see my own shadow from the side of the wall up to the ceiling part.

My shadow was gone. I opened my eyes widely with panic. I checked the entire room. Still was not able to see my shadow. Despite all of that, I still could hear my sisters and cousins' voices outdoors from the opened window while they were playing. My dog barked from time to time. I was still in panic mode.

Then all of a sudden, my mom called me for dinner. As I was leaving the room, my shadow had returned, and it followed to the exit of the room from where I went to the living room to eat my dinner with the rest of the members.

I had finished my dinner. Felt full. I decided to breathe in the windy, a bit cool summer night's air. I went out to the yard of the house. The yard was designed with brown-bricked fences around it. I went to the corner of the fence, sat down. My dog came to me wagging its tail. He was large

Kangal Shepherd dog. He had dark eyes with gray thick fur. When he barked, the whole neighborhood, even from the far distance, could hear him. This kind of breed is good for guarding the house. I went to buy that dog with my grandpa when he was still a small cute puppy. I liked him from the way he looked at me wagging his small tail, opening his mouth, showing a dog's smiling gesture. He sat next to me. I petted him. At that time, everyone was already inside the house. The cool wind blew, the tree's leaves were shaking passively. I inhaled a deep breath, gazed up. The night sky was full of stars. My back leaned on the wall while sitting, my head up, still gazing at the sky. I can't recall how long I sat in that position.

By the time I moved a little bit, I realized Bax, my dog, had left my side, pacing around the house, sniffing the ground. I checked my phone to see the time, 8:58 P.M. I sighed. The moment I tried to get up, I received a new Messenger notification. It was already the 2nd message notification. The message was sent by Ratanaporn. I sat back and thought a lot. My feelings were in a lost. I did not know what is right and what is wrong. Was it right to never reply to her again after she ghosted me? Was it wrong not to reply to it? My heart despaired, kind of hurt. It seemed to me so tranquil that I heard my heart beat slowly. Eventually, with some hesitations, I made up my mind not to reply. I got up, went straight to my room. I took a shower, as the weather was warm, I changed into just a t-shirt and underwear. I crawled into my bed and started looking at the ceiling again. The room was completely dark, the only weak light came from our yard's right corner. I couldn't think of anything. My thoughts were full of Ratanaporn. I couldn't hold myself, took my phone, and opened her earlier texts.

"Hello, Daler. I hope you are doing well. I hope everything is fine with you. I was absent from our previous chat; I couldn't keep my word and didn't text you back. I am not sure how you felt about that kind of action. I really enjoyed chatting you at that time. I felt good. I seriously wanted to continue as soon as I was done with my stuff. I don't even know why I am explaining all these things to you, maybe because my heart is telling me to do so. Something devastating happened. I was not able to talk to anyone at school for some time. I kept myself isolated in my room. We received news that my beloved grandma passed away. She was my father's mom. My father bought tickets instantly to his hometown. We flew back that winter time. We stayed there for a couple of weeks, then pulled ourselves together, accepted the loss of one of our dearest family members, and flew back to States. She was 66; I consider it still a young age to die. Doctors couldn't comprehend why she died at that not-old age. She was in good healthy condition. It happened out of nothing. She just slept in her bed to never wake up again. She always loved to cook for us (her beloved grandchildren) and took great care of us. Words cannot describe her kindness. Over 1,000 people gathered at her funeral to mourn for her. She was such an important person for our family. Ah, if that death wouldn't have occurred, I am certain we would continue chatting every day up until now. Daler, I hope you understand me. Thank you."

I read the text twice. My heart felt better that she felt good chatting with me. On the other hand, I sympathized with her that such an event happened to her family. Before giving her my full response, I opened her second message.

"Daler, I myself wouldn't feel like replying back to the person who would ghost me for such a long time. To tell you the truth, I am willing to chat with you more often. Although our time zones have a big gap, I am sure we will find the solution to chat more, at any case. Hope to receive your reply!

Sincerely,
Ratanaporn Saetang."

"Of course, I will reply to you, with no doubts!" I said to myself and proceeded to type the reply to her.

"Hey Ratanaporn... First of all, I am really sorry to hear that. You are a strong-spirited girl who went through these difficult moments. May she rest in peace, amen!
"I am flattered that you felt good chatting with me. It is my pleasure. I must say, I feel the same way about you as well. I feel that connection too. Honestly, I was a bit frustrated. I thought that you would never text me back. Please don't feel bad about that. I completely understand you now. I was wrong for being frustrated.
"But here we are, texting again. I am so happy right now, at this moment, texting you.

"Certainly, I want to chat with you every day. Yes, we will find a solution for sure, no doubt about that. I will make sure that we will stay in touch as much as we can, as long as we can." To my surprise, she saw my text in a few seconds right after she received it. Yet again, she didn't reply instantly, was left on seen. I didn't get mad about it this time. I just made up my mind to wait and see what happens. Stress was gone; I closed my eyes, was dead to the world.

China

I met Ju in one of my classes during the first semester of my university. She usually wore oversized T-shirts with a skirt and sneakers on her feet, sometimes with different-colored bucket hats too. She was petite, with big breasts and slim body shape. She had big, brown, attractive eyes with short blonde hair.

We had a subject called Environmental Science, and our tutor had allocated a few groups for a big project that would impact our final scores for the completion of the subject successfully. I was in the same group as Ju. If we had never been in the same group, with my anxiety about talking to girls, I would have never approached her, not to mention dating. Was it luck? Maybe yes. We had group meetings every Thursday until it was our time to give the project's presentation. Our group consisted of four members: two Indian senior girls, myself, and Ju, who were still freshmen. Unlike Ju and me, those two Indian girls discussed almost all the issues regarding our preparation. I involved myself from time to time, but Ju didn't speak unless someone asked for her opinion on some matters. The Indian girls were seemed to be irritated by my lesser activity than them. From my side, I always did my best. They even once asked Ju to be more active; she looked careless, not showing many expressions. I wondered if most Chinese girls had similar cultural expressions.

On our 3rd week of group meetings, I decided to be a little bit closer, making a bold move. We usually ended our meetings by the evening. I went straight to the food court to eat my dinner. The place was nearby my campus, only 3–4 minutes of walking distance. So, after the meeting was over, I asked her whether she would join me for dinner at the food court. The two Indian girls left our side at the exit of the meeting room. The perfect moment had been given to me.

"Ju," I said with a lower, nervous tone of voice. "Would you love to join me for dinner at the food court now?" She looked into my eyes with an expressionless face. "Ok," she responded without any question. "That's great, let's go!" I said cheerfully with a smile; she still showed no reaction at all. We just walked towards the food court, side by side in silence. I had a hard time thinking of what kind of topics I would talk to her about while eating. Besides that, it was my first-ever dinner with a girl. Sweat kept falling down my temples; she didn't care to notice that, just looked straight ahead until we entered the food court. That evening she wore a white skirt with two different colors of sneakers, pink and white. She wore a pink oversized shirt on top. I thought that kind of style suited her round face, with a small nose and black thin eyebrows.

We entered the place.

"What do you want to eat?" I asked her. She stood, thought for a moment. "Hmm, I don't want to eat these fast-food meals right now. I don't feel like it. Let's go to my place and order some Chinese meal." It was the first, longest line of speaking I ever heard from her. Without any thoughts, I agreed immediately. "Alright, let's do it," I said enthusiastically. She looked at me, nodded, and we exited the food court.

Little did I know that she drove a car? We came to the parking, got in her big SUV Lexus LX car. For the small girl like her, she drove such an enormous car. I was honestly astonished. The interior of the car was too cozy, vast, had soft leathered seats. She started the engine, vroom, slowly pushed the pedal, the car moved away from the parking.

"So, where do you live?" I asked her. It took her some time to react to my question as she was focused on driving. She responded without looking at me. "Amm, Meadows." As far as my knowledge, that area had villas, wealthy people lived there. From the moment I saw her car, it had become obvious to me that she was wealthy. "Oh, nice place," I said. But she gave me zero reaction that time. We were already at the J.L.T. area. She stopped her car near the Chinese restaurant in that area. "I changed my mind, let's eat at this restaurant first. The meal that I am going to buy for you is not good for the delivery," she explained to me reluctantly. "But I will take you to my place for the drink," she said then with a smile. I couldn't refuse. So, I agreed and followed her without any arguments. "Alright," I said, nodding my head. Next, we entered the restaurant. One of the hostesses greeted us. Ju talked to her in Mandarin, in which I had zero knowledge. The traditional Chinese lanterns on a spherical shape hung from the ceiling of the restaurant. The walls were covered with some images of pandas. Straight ahead, a large dragon's image decorated the end of the restaurant's wall. The walls were covered in red. This type of design shows some of Chinese important traditions and culture. One amazing feature about that restaurant was that each table was covered with a small, thin wooden mini wall. It was kind of a private table. The hostess took us to the end of the right corner's table. There were two small comfortable seats. We sat across from each other. The waiter approached our table and asked about our orders. First, he spoke to Ju; she ordered a meal. Again, I didn't understand a word, sat there dumbfounded. The waiter left our sight at the end, looking and giving me a smile. "He didn't talk to you because I ordered a big Chinese traditional meal for the two of us," she explained to me.

"What is the meal?" I asked.

"It's a Hot-Pot."

"What is Hot-Pot?"

"It's a Chinese traditional meal."

"Yeah, I understood about that point. But what is it made of?"

"You'll see!" she said.

Silence seized the moment between us. I noticed something unfamiliar on the table. It contained a round, circled glassed shape in the middle. I pointed that shape out and asked her, "What is it for? I have never seen such things at any restaurants before."

"It's the heater for the Hot-Pot."

"Oh, I see." I became more curious about that Hot-Pot meal. I assumed that I learned one feature about her—she changes her mind quickly about circumstances, like the one, bringing me to the restaurant. But maybe I was wrong. Minutes passed in a silence again. At last, the waiter came. I thought he brought our meal, but instead, he brought around a 30-centimetre sized big pot. He gently put the pot on that circled glass of our table. The pot had two sides on it One side had plain water, the other had red-colored water on it. Next, he brought two smaller bowls with chopsticks, and one fork.

"Now, it's time to heat the pot. This water is for non-spicy, and this red is for spicy heat. You can heat and eat the meals either way you want it," she cheerfully told me.

"Ohh, it all makes sense now. I see!" I said with a surprised expression on my face. She nodded in response and began to proceed to heat the glass and boil the water. "The waiter will start bringing different types of meals and vegetables. I will teach you how to eat with chopsticks. If you fail many times, just give up at the end; you can eat with that fork that I told him to bring for you in case. But I will make sure you eat it with chopsticks!"

"Thank you; would really appreciate that. It will be interesting to eat with chopsticks." She smiled. The waiter brought several plates with different kinds of meals and vegetables. One plate contained thinly sliced meat, the other contained sliced potatoes, the other had dumplings, some had leaf vegetables, and shrimps on another plate. I was bewildered if we would be able to eat that much.

"Wow, are you sure we can eat all of it?"

"Why not? We are two, and I am pretty hungry right now."

"Alright then, let's give it a go!" First, she put dumplings and shrimps into the spicy side for her herself.

"So, you want it spicy as well?" she asked with an interested look.

"Hmm, I am not sure. I will try it out. Put some on the bland side too." She mixed it up. "You know, I am eager to eat spicy potatoes. Can you put some too?"

"Okay, but we have to wait until the dumplings and shrimps are fully cooked. Then I will do it."

"Alright, understood." While the meals were cooking, I decided to ask some question about her. "So, what part of **China** are you from?"

"Fujian, Fuzhou."

"Hmm. What part of China is it located?"

She gave me a short answer again. "Southeastern."

"Do you have siblings?"

"What is siblings?" she asked with surprise. I didn't want to judge her and explained in detail.

"It means having a brother or sister."

"No, I am the only child. My mom was pregnant. I was supposed to have a sister. But due to the Chinese strict ONE CHILD policy, she had to have an abortion. Even if she gave birth, my parents would have to pay huge amounts of money every month for breaking the law. In those days, they didn't have much money. On top of that, my dad didn't want to fight with the government as it would be useless and waste of his money and time. He saw his friends and neighbors suffering because of that issue. He told me that lots of people were leaving our province for the U.S., illegally. Numbers of them were caught, deported back to my homeland. As a result of that, they were punished and imprisoned for betraying our country. Their families had faced bad consequences. So my dad didn't want to take this kind of risk for his family. Of course, my parents were disheartened after the abortion, but that was best for the safety of our family. I was a little girl, I still remember it; my mom wept for months. Eventually, with her strength, she managed to bear the pain, overcame it with our family's strong bond."

"What a story!"

"Yes… Oh look, shrimps and dumplings are ready." She took them out and asked me to pass my bowl. I passed, and she put mixed with spicy and bland. But she put only spicy ones for herself. She slowly put all the potatoes on the spicy side. "Oh damn, I completely forgot to order drinks!" she said. A waiter was passing by serving the other table. She called him. It was the same waiter. She ordered in Mandarin first for herself, then asked me. "What do you want?"

"Amm, just a coke." She muttered to him; he nodded and left our side. "Done, he'll be here in a minute." Indeed, as she said, he returned really fast, bringing a can of beer and a coke for me. "Oh, so you will drink a beer?"

"Yes, don't worry; it's nothing," she said winking at me. She then continued. "Let's start eating."

As we unhurriedly began eating, she initiated her teachings on how to use chopsticks. "Now, watch me and listen to me at the same time." I watched her attentively. "First, you pick up one chopstick, place it between your index and thumb fingers, and connect. Then, grip the second one with your index and thumb fingers again. Lastly, practice opening and closing the chopsticks. Here, like this." She showed how to use it, then grabbed one of her spicy dumplings and put it in her mouth. "See, easy," she said, munching on the dumpling in her mouth. I did my best to follow her instructions. I held two of them, but when I tried to grab dumplings, they kept falling. "No, no, watch," she said and showed me again how to do it. I tried again and again, kept failing. From my last attempt, I finally picked one up successfully, but when it was close to my mouth, it fell down on my knees, making my gray shorts dirty. She grinned and spoke up. "Actually, you did not do that bad for the first timer. You should keep practicing; you will be a pro eventually. Now, you must eat using that fork. Otherwise, your food will get cold."

"Yeah, you are right." Then I started to eat those dumplings. The bland dumplings, which I tried first, tasted sweet and a bit crispy. Then I tried the spicy one too. Both of the dumplings were made with beef meat. I liked the spicy one as well. But the aftermath was bad; my mouth started burning, and the taste perception was gone when I drank my coke. She saw me suffering.

"Relax, the burn goes away in a matter of a few seconds. When you eat spicy, you must not mix it with bland ones immediately; instead, keep eating spicy, wait, then eat the non-spicy. Hence, your taste receptors on your tongue will be back, and you can perceive the taste again."

"Okay, understood. Honestly, I liked it. Maybe when I get used to it, I will eat spicy food more often than in the past." We finished the dumplings and shrimps. As much as I liked spicy dumplings, somehow it didn't go the same with spicy shrimps. She kept eating one after another. "Potatoes are ready," she said and took my bowl to put some for me as well. Lastly, she asked me whether or not I want spicy meat and leaf vegetables too. "Do you want them spicy too, or mixed?"

"Hmm, let's make them spicy too. Are you okay with it?" I asked, thinking.

"I am down for spicy too," she responded and put vegetables with meat on the pot's spicy side. Afterwards, it was time to eat our spicy potatoes. It tasted good; the burn on my mouth wasn't that strong as with previous meals. It made me wonder, was it because I already got used to it, or the spiciness on potatoes didn't have much of an effect. We kept eating, just smiling at each other and enjoying our dinner. While eating potatoes, she ordered the second can of a beer. I became worried. "How you will drive after drinking two cans already?"

"Huh, don't worry, my dear. I can have seven to ten cans and still drive like a sober person. Calm down," she told me.

"Wow, that's impressive!" She smirked in response.

By the time we finished up our whole dinner, she had six cans. True, she looked as if nothing had happened—sober, completely alive, and as active as a human being can be. I tried to pay for the dinner, but she hushed me down and paid the entire bill. I always thought that it was illegal to sell alcohol at restaurants in Dubai.

On our way to her car, I decided to ask her about it. Then she explained to me, "You are right at one point. But restaurants can still serve alcohol as long as they have a license for it. In addition, a person must be 21 or over."

"21," I thought. How come she could be 21 if she told me that she is a freshman, just like me? As she was driving us to her place, it struck me that she drove so vigilantly. It kind of surprised me that she had so much focus despite drinking. I didn't make any final assumptions because people are different. I even heard that some people can drink a full bottle of vodka and still be sober as if nothing has been consumed or touched their organs. Zero effect, period. I decided not to disturb her focus while driving and looked through the window. I had never noticed such a phenomenon. The moon shaped on its full size, having a light orange color. Oddly enough, I enjoyed that view just by staring at it until we reached her location. "Are you okay?" she called me, shaking my left shoulder. "Oh, yeah, yeah, I am good."

"You looked like a zombie losing his mind, staring at those buildings and passing cars. It made me a bit worried and—"

"All is good. Please do not worry. I just saw something beautiful," I interrupted and assured her.

"Alright, as you say. Anyways, we are here. This is the house I live in," she told me, pointing at the closed dark window.

We got off the car. She unlocked the door, and we stepped into her house. She switched all the lights on. "Should I take off my shoes?" I asked her.

"No need for that. Come on, follow me." A few meters away from the straight hall that we walked down, on the left side was a light-grayed Lawson sofa. "Please sit on the sofa and wait for me. I will take a quick bath and be right back," she politely asked me. I nodded, sat down on the sofa. The seat was cushioned, maximizing softness. Indeed, I felt comfortable sitting on it. The big TV screen was attached to the wall in front of the sofa. Two similarly designed couches were placed on both sides of the sofa. I moved my head to the left and saw a table with wheels, set down with black leathered three slipper chairs. I marveled at what that was for. I noticed the tinted window that I saw upon entering the house from the car. A small bookshelf was positioned behind one of the table's chairs with some small framed photos laid down on it. Perhaps these photos were from some of her memorable events. I leaned back, relaxed for a bit, stretching my arms up. A sudden long burp came out of my mouth. It had an unbearable rotten spiced smell, which disgusted me. I put my palm close to my mouth to check my breath. I blew the air onto my palm; the air didn't hit in the direction of my nose. I did it one more time, still couldn't smell anything. I made the final attempt, no result. I sighed and gave up. "As long as I don't sit too close to her, I hope she won't notice my current bad breath," I muttered anxiously.

She returned, sat next to me, wearing a plain white nightgown with pink slippers.

"Hey, listen, make yourself at home. If you want to go to the bathroom, go ahead," she told me, assuring me.

"Yeah, you are right, I really need to go to the toilet now." She smiled at me, showing me the way to the bathroom. I felt so relieved taking a long piss.

By the time I came back, she held two cans of beers in her hands. "You are already grown up, here, have some."

"Oh, I have never drunk alcohol before. And I can't return home drunk."

"Don't you worry about that; you can stay overnight at my place. I am here for you," she said, winking at me, then handed me one can. We opened our cans. I sipped, tasted bitterness in my mouth, and swallowed it hardly. She grinned at me. "Come on, it is not that bad, ha ha."

"First time, as you said earlier about getting used to something. I am sure if I have a few more cans, the scenario will be better," I said, sipping some more.

She nodded. "By the way, the restaurant staff knows me already as I am their regular customer. Therefore, you didn't see me showing my ID to them. Why would I show my ID to any other places too? I am 24 already. Do I look like a minor? I don't think so," she told me, rolling her eyes. I noticed her nipples through her thin nightgown.

"Oh really? I thought you are 18 as well. We are on the same course, first semester!"

She shook her head. "Not everyone who is in their first semester must be 18. Some people work, save money, then enter the university. Some raise their families, et cetera, et cetera. In my case, I wanted to have one more degree in some foreign place where I would study my subjects in English. I can see you are narrow-minded. No offense."

"None taken. I understand. You can help me to broaden my mind too."

"Good. Sure!"

My phone rang. It was my dad calling me to ask what time I would come back home. I tried to convince him by telling him that I had a big upcoming project for my group, that all of our group mates would stay at one of our mate's homes overnight. He didn't mind much. It would play out differently if I talked to my mom. Since my mom and sisters were still in my hometown, I got away with it easily. "Sorry, my dad called me. Since he allowed me, I can freely stay at your place tonight."

"Good boy," she said in response.

Silence caught the moment. We finished our first cans. She unhurriedly got up, leaving my side. She came back with two more cans and handed me one. I opened it and decided to ask her few questions. "So… um… what is your first degree?"

"Arts in Human Behavioral Psychology."

"That's interesting."

"Sure it is," she said with a smile. I smiled back. I sipped my beer. "I assume you had to take English extra classes because your English is so good," I told her, praising.

"Not at all. I just learned by watching movies, online video tutorials. In addition, the high school that I went to was strict with their English language classes. Lots of students failed to get the high school diploma because of that. They took the exams several times. Bottom line, after finishing that school, I already had the basics. Remember, when you learn basics and start practicing a lot, you will learn quicker and more efficiently. People complicate things, but in my personal opinion, everything is as simple as that," she sighed and had her sip. I nodded without saying anything. She quickly chugged her whole can, got up, brought six more cans, and put them beside us on the sofa. She sighed and spoke. "Ah, I won't have to keep getting up, so I brought some more."

"Yeah, I can see that, smart move." She looked into my eyes for a second, then asked me.

"Wanna know some psychology about girls, their needs, their behaviors…? I am pretty certain you will need that kind of knowledge for your future!"

"Yes, that would be lovely," I responded.

She sipped, took a deep breath, gathered all her emotions, and then began her preach.

"First of all, I want to let you know one important thing. I am sharing all this information with you… you know, you look like Chinese. Not too specifically like Chinese, but overall, like an Asian. If you go to Southeast Asia, they will consider you as their own for sure." I wasn't surprised by that because she wasn't the first person to tell me that. So, I just smiled and nodded.

She hit the backseat of the sofa with her elbow. Her boobs bounced when she did that. Then she furiously kept on. "Ah, nowadays most of the men have been so feminized, ugh… I can't stand it. It is not that hard to understand a girl. All we want is security, protection, and love, nothing more. I talked to many Western people, made some friends when I traveled to Los Angeles. The guys complained to me that their wives cheated on them no matter how much they loved them. Duh, that's because they never felt protected by you, because you never acted like a real man. You have to have responsibility for your actions. I will explain some rules."

"First of all, when your girl gets angry, don't fight back. Girls are fragile. Just come to her, hug her, pet her, and kiss her. She will and feel much more secure.

"Secondly, a man should take dominance. A man should make the decisions. It is not in our nature to develop masculinity. Once we forcibly develop it because of a man being cuckolded, a man loses his worth to us. We do what we want to do, like dating as much as we want, and lots of other stuff.

"Third and most important, love the girl. But don't overshow it; take actions most of the time…" While listening to her, I started losing balance in my head. The first-ever dizziness hit my head. Yet, it felt good. Silence fell over us. I chugged my third can, opened the fourth, and sipped it. All along, she narrowed her eyes, staring at the floor. "I have found good in you; my guts cued me to trust in you. You must remember these facts for your own good. This is a good advantage for you, for your future. Promise me?" she asked me, caring about me. I nodded and said with assurance. "I promise you, Ju."

"Good boy! I am certain you will have many more experiences to learn even more. Don't be shy, explore as much as you can. Have that wisdom before getting married. Your wife will be lucky." I acknowledged her and kept sipping my beer. She continued. "You see, when a girl loses her virginity with the wrong man, moreover, then breaks up with him... we feel regret. We feel like losing our preciousness, our dignity. Unlike the boys, they feel proud. It brings them more confidence. I still don't understand these phenomena. Perhaps these are essential differences between feminism and masculinity. However, many people would debate with me about such things," she let out a big sigh, then kept on. "I myself held the regret for 2 years. I lost my innocence at the age of 16. I fell in love, had my innocent naive trust in that guy, then poof, he broke up with me. I can't tell how much pain I bore for those 2 years. I couldn't do anything but accept it. I have been certain about that phenomenon because most of my friends felt the same way when they lost their virginity to the wrong person." She chugged her sixth can, opened the seventh, sipped it, and said with a smile. "Despite having that repentance, with the current knowledge that I have now, I am confident that I will be able to find the right man to get married." I smiled back at her with more dizziness. "I am certain you will."

She kept chugging. "So, Ju, tell me about your family. Why did you decide to study specifically in Dubai?" I asked with curiosity.

"That's a good question. Thanks to my father's hard work in my hometown, he met many good people and developed a great network. Some of his friends advised him to expand in the Middle East. He opened restaurants in Qatar, Kuwait, Saudi Arabia, and here in the U.A.E. He opened two to three branches in major cities of those countries. There are two branches in Dubai; one of them is the one we had dinner at earlier, and the other one is located in Deira. There are two branches in cities such as Abu Dhabi, Sharjah, and Ras Al Khaimah."

I broke in. "Wow, so the restaurant we ate at was your father's!" She grinned and nodded while sipping her beer. She carried on. "Frankly speaking, I am still not sure why I chose to study here. Maybe it's just for trial. I really don't sense any student life here; it's pretty boring. Boring lectures, some incompetent students, although you are one of the good ones I met. Or am I too old, that I lost that sense... don't know. Probably I will transfer to the Australian campus and see how it goes there. In fact, let me just finish this semester. Maybe I will give it a go to still continue... don't know," she told me, constantly changing her mind.

By the time she finished her can, all the cans were already consumed. "Let me show you the Mahjong game, but first, let me grab some more cans," she said.

She came to me holding cans of beer in both of her hands, then showed me the way to the wheeled table with chairs that I noticed earlier. We sat across from each other. Before she spoke to me, I did a quick observation. There were tiles with some different Chinese symbols laid on the table. It reminded me of dominoes but in a Chinese way. Of course, there's a big difference between them.

She began explaining the game to me. "Look at these symbols. It is really easy to play the game. Each player exchanges tiles, and as soon as one player has 14 tiles that match each other, the winner is declared, and the game ends, thus called 'Mahjong'." While I did my best to absorb each word that she interpreted for me with my dizziness, she opened her can, literally chugged it in a few seconds, and sighed. "Oh shoot, there must be at least 3 players for the game to be played, which would make sense. We are only two." She put her palms on her head, showing a little bit of embarrassment. She looked straight at my face. "Hey, you don't look so good. Are you alright?"

"Yes, I am," I said, giving a loud burp. "Ohh, shit, sorry," I said apologetically. "But the good news is, you are alright," she responded, ignoring my burp.

I felt discomfort after showing that, but I couldn't blame myself for not controlling myself. I had an excuse because I was drunk. I am pretty sure she didn't mind that at all.

"You need to lie down. Come on, get up, we'll go to my room." She pulled me up from my seat, handed me a few cans at the same time holding some in her hands too, then we headed to her room. I hardly made steps up to the second floor of her house.

She opened the door to her room. Right in front of the room was a glassed wall with a small door and a balcony. The curtains were pulled on the end side of it, close to her bed. A small TV was attached to the wall straight from the bed's view. The bedside table looked empty, nothing placed on it. So she proceeded to place all of our cans on it. She asked me to sit on the bed. I did as she told me to. I sat; arms touched on the sheet behind my body with a woozy head. She slowly sat on my lap. She put her arms around my shoulder, started petting my head, and kissed on my forehead.

"You are a really kind-hearted guy; I literally feel it. I want to make this night special for you. Your first magic night!" she said, whispering in my ears while petting me at the same time. I felt the softness of her butt on my lap, and an erection came into the action. My penis woke up, getting hard.

"Now, lie down, put your head on the pillow," she said, giving me a second kiss on my forehead. During those minutes, I didn't say a word and obeyed her commands. I passively moved myself to the pillow's side, lied down on my back with my arms to the side, placing my head on the pillow. I saw the glimmering ceiling. My eyes kept blurring, and having clear sight as well, mixing it all up simultaneously. She asked me to close my eyes completely while standing on the side of the bed. I did as she told me. A moment passed, I felt something on my legs. She kept whispering to me not to open my eyes. All of a sudden, I felt warm wet sucking in my penis. She kept silent, and at last when I couldn't hold myself, I opened my eyes. My shorts and underwear were off; I saw her head moving up and down, sucking my penis, totally naked. It felt great. It was like masturbating, but someone else doing it for you with a much better version. A few minutes passed; I experienced one of the best-relaxed moments in my entire life. I groaned, closing my eyes after an ejaculation in her mouth. I can't recall how long it took me to be in the relaxed mode with my eyes shut; when I opened my eyes again, she was getting on top of me. I noticed a tattoo under the left side of her breast with the written sign of 'DADDY'S LITTLE MONSTER'. I didn't bother asking her what that meant. My eyes automatically stared at her oval-shaped pink nipples. The next thing, she penetrated my penis in her warm tight vagina. She began her mission, moving her body, shaking, giving me all the best pleasure that I could ever have. Her tits were bouncing, I grabbed them, squeezed them, and massaged her nipples with my thumbs.

She pulled out, a second ejaculation occurred. Thus, I lost my virginity on that magical night that stay in my memories for ages.

Friday

Friday, the first day of the weekend in the U.A.E. Although I cannot recall the exact day, it was late in September of 2015. At about 8 P.M. in the evening, I went to the Jumeirah Lakes Tower Park. The park had vast grasslands along with green-leaved trees, placed chairs, and a basketball playground. I visited the park for the first time.

I took the metro, which was only one station away from my area, then walked towards the park. I bought a large bottle of cold orange juice from the supermarket on my way. As the weather had high humidity even at nights in Fall, making me sweat, I enjoyed every sip of my juice. I strolled among tall modern-designed buildings. The roof lights of the buildings were flickering through the night airglow. To my knowledge, those flickering lights of the tall buildings are designed to signal airplane pilots, so they would see the lights of the building to have a clear vision of the particular city. It hugely decreases chances of an accidental vision crash. Pretty safe to say that a person who came up with such an idea is a genius.

The park was quite crowded. I sat on the grass nearby the basketball ground. Some people were picnicking, some were watching the game, and some were playing badminton—typical weekend activities. I sipped my juice, checked the bottle; it had already been half empty. The bottle sweated, getting hot and making my juice warm and untasty. At least it was still something; it kept my mouth out of dryness, passively killing my thirstiness. The heated wind was breezing the environment, making everyone around sweat bit by bit. The sky looked cloudless with a few barely visible stars. I wondered how people played games in such high humid hot weather.

According to science, our body is flexible. Wherever we go, our body, our immune system adapts to the specific environment we are in. However, not everyone's immune system is capable of adapting. But the majority of a healthy population has a high chance of getting used to new things. These kinds of thoughts made me stop being surprised. Maybe they enjoyed and played intensively because they are used to this environment. In any case, my mind started wondering about different sort of things. Some philosophical thoughts about life struck my mind with deep questions included.

We are born, we live our lives. Some are poor, some are average, some are rich, and some are mega-rich. Some die early, some die after living a long life. What do we do here, dwelling on Earth? What is our purpose in life? These are complicated questions, yet simple.

There are people living purposeless empty lives. There are opposites of them who figured out how to live and be successful in their lives. I have no idea about myself. As of now, I am just a freshman, studying Bachelor of Commerce, Finance. They say you will always find jobs with such a degree. Even if I won't be able to find any job in the future,

I can join my dad for his Real Estate business. Although it bores me, I won't have any other choices. It's better to be active doing something than sitting at home wasting time by doing nothing.

Why are so many afraid of failure? What I have learned from the books of sages is that unless you fail at something, you won't gain anything. You will either take it as negativity, be miserable for life, or see positive things from it—learning, learning new things for experiences for your own good. We make mistakes; nothing is perfect on this planet. No matter how much of a perfectionist you try to be, there will always be a hole in something about you. As in Japanese wisdom, accept Wabi Sabi. That means accepting imperfection in life. I have made lots of mistakes in my short current life, one of them being trusting friends. I have learned that regardless of how close that person is, you have to keep some secrets about yourself that only you know for the rest of your life.

I have always been fascinated by how our planet is created. We see clouds, clear sky, the sun, and even the moon during the daytime. We see stars, sometimes night clouds, the moon itself in its different shapes. We experience lots of seasonal weather in different places. The most thing that always fascinated me was sunrise and sunset. I am curious. Are we supposed to get up at sunrise and go to bed at sunset? Isn't that the purpose of this day and night phenomenon? Even if an average person would try to keep up with this kind of schedule, I bet it would be hard to get enough sleep and energy to do the daily routines—going for 9–5 jobs, being married, having kids, having obligations to pay the bills, etc., etc. This system that we live in seems complicated, yet it can be as simple as that. Do I want that kind of life, working 9–5 until I retire? They say it is good for security. When you retire, you can get the proper pension from the government. I heard that system works well in the West and East of Asia. But what if I want to be an entrepreneur? I would open my own company, as my dad has his Real Estate business. I could go for another kind of business, maybe a restaurant. I don't know. I am going to see what will happen in the future because every year, my vision keeps changing. Probably I will have clarity if I meet many people, broaden my mind. Yeah, it sounds like a good idea. I remember my grandfather used to preach one thing: "Be a Leader." Be a leader in your life. Be a leader for your company. Be a leader among your friends; he preached to me every time I visited our grandparents with my mom and my sisters. But what does it mean to be a great leader? Perhaps, by living my life, paying attention to details, I will find out the true meaning of it. As of now, I haven't practiced the leadership skills at all. Maybe studying at my current university, I will have some clarity about it. While having such conceptions in my head, I realized my juice had been all warmed up. I decided to chug the whole bottle before the taste had gotten even worse. This time the taste wasn't that bad. Was it because my mouth dried out and I needed fluidity for my organs, and it gave me self-deceptions? Anyhow, my thoughts kept striking me again and again. We live only once on this planet, they say. Life is too short, they say. Live your life to the fullest, they say. Enjoy your life, they say. Don't waste your time on bullshits, they say. But what bullshits are? Perhaps some important things in life are bullshits for someone but vital for someone else, and vice versa. Don't judge people, they say. That is true because I can't judge anyone without knowing anything about what is going on behind the scenes. Did I judge somebody hard before? I don't think so. I was just a quiet kid, minding my own business. All I did most of the time in my senior school years is to focus on my studies and go home; I barely even wanted to communicate. But I have new hopes now. I hope I can make decent foreign friends. My dad didn't just bring me to study here. I suppose he wanted to give me the experience of new surroundings, new cultures.

Why do nations have wars? Why do people kill each other? What causes all these horrible genocides? Why do people want so much power? We live here temporarily; a person dies at any cost, at any time. This is an inevitable phenomenon for our lives. This is a pure fact that every person knows about it. Yet, despite knowing all these facts, people still hunger for more and more power, acquiring territories.

Watching all those people who conquered lands, they perished, and civilizations have been changing for centuries. The conquered lands kept dividing for centuries. Yes, those who conquered—their names have been marked on human histories. But still… why did they embark on such conquests, knowing that they would die anyway? For what? It is another fact throughout histories that empires fade away, new generations are born, new rules are always set, new visions, etc., etc.

Why do people have fears? Is it in our nature? I am scared myself of lots of things. I am scared of standing on the edge of heights. My legs shake; I feel like on the verge of dying. I think we can't control our fears. Some fears come from our DNA. Yes, of course, there are achievable things, but I doubt that born fears can ever be overcome.

Why do people love sex so much? Why does it drive people crazy? Does it feel so good? Is it the best pleasure in our lives? There are even tons of horrible news concerning sex rapes. Oh my God, this is insane. Why is this desire for sex so out of control? Man, it is too hard to understand. Maybe I am still too young to understand many things. I know one important thing: by having sex, people make babies, bringing new generations. Other than that, I really don't understand the high desire for it. Damn, I myself have never been drawn to sex that much. At my current age, my lust for sex is supposed to be at a peak level. Is it in my DNA not to have a high-level lust for sex? I feel kind of ashamed to ask such questions from my parents. I guess I will have to figure this out on my own from my future experiences. However, I have no clear vision of my future. Possibly my life would be boring. Possibly my life would be interesting. Well, I am interested myself in what will happen in my future. Let it be. Eh, it is a real brain drain to overthink about my future life. On top of it all, I couldn't fathom why different kinds of notions were wandering in my mind. Until that moment, I never had such an odd experience. If you can say that it is odd, tastes differ. Different people, different opinions, different assumptions. But I had a few assumptions myself, whether they are wrong or right. Was it because of some hormonal changes? Was it because I wanted something new? But never knew how to gain it. Or maybe because I felt lonely, didn't make new friends upon having my new semester so far? Who knows!

I had mixed feelings. I shook my head sitting on that grass. Meanwhile, sweat streamed down from my temples. My butt hurt from sitting still, so I moved it a little bit, to circulate the blood in it. I vaguely continued watching the basketball game a few meters away from me. A stranger came to my side, speaking to me in some foreign language which I had no idea about, but he looked Asian. I had never seen an Asian with such a facial structure. His eyes were more convex with thicker irises, a smaller lens vault, and narrower angles. It slightly looked like Chinese eyes with similar iris and angle parameters. He had a long undercut ponytail hairstyle with a goatee beard. His physical shape made me assume that he had been working out for years. He was wearing Nike slim white T-shirt with Nike purple shorts and Air Jordan sneakers. By his outfit, I concluded that he is fan of famous sports brands. He carried a dark-colored parcel on his left hand on which I was not able to see what was there inside of it. When he said his first words, I felt dumbfounded without getting any of it. Then he spoke again by asking me.

"Kabayan?"

"Excuse me?" I asked him back, being lost. He spoke to me something which I had not understood a word for the third time. I shook my head. Then at last, he started speaking in English. "So you are not Kabayan?" he asked again. I gave me him a firm no, shaking my head. "Nope."

"Ah, alright, I see. By the way, you look like Asian. I thought you are Pinoy, that's why I was trying to talk to you in Tagalog," he told me.

I wasn't surprised, though, that he told me that I look like an Asian person; it wasn't the first time. I got curious and asked him, "What is Kabayan?"

He smiled and responded, "If a person is from the Philippines, we call our fellow Filipino or Filipina Kabayans. Also, that indicates that you are from the same country. Does that make sense?" I nodded.

"May I sit next to you?" he asked me politely. I didn't mind that. "Yeah, sure." He placed his parcel with three bottles of water beside himself, then sat next to my right side. "What is your name?" he asked me.

"Daler. And yours?"

"Call me Randy."

"Gotchu! Nice to meet you."

"Pleased to meet you too, Daler," he said with a smile, and we shook hands. He watched the basketball game for a second, then thinking about something, asked me. "Hey, by the way, do you want some water? I got three bottles in my parcel." I looked at him and said with my sweated face.

"I have just finished the juice, but yeah, I could have some water as well. This weather has been making me thirsty, no matter how much liquid I consume. Thank you." He handed me one big bottle of water then responded.

"It's good to drink juice, but it will not quench your thirst regardless of how much you consume, especially in this kind of weather in this former deserted place. Sugared drinks can never quench your thirst; on the contrary, the more you drink them, the more you will want them, like a drug," he chuckled then went on. "It's the way to make money for the soft drink companies. Water is the holy grail. First of all, when you consume it, it is highly beneficial for your health. Second, it quenches your thirst for good." I listened to what he had explained to me carefully, chugged loads of my water bottle, and then made an assumption. "Seeing your physique, I can say you are into sports a lot."

He gave me a smile and said. "Indeed, you are right. On top of that, I am a professional fitness coach. I have been working out since my teenage years, fell in love with this sport, and then made up my mind to turn into a professional coach. I have plans to open my own gym in future."

"Wow, that's amazing. Sounds like a great plan." He nodded and smiled.

"I love basketball too. Are you into any sports?"

"Never been a big fan of any. I am watching this game now and have no idea about the rules, just blankly watching it."

"Sports are good for a lifetime, especially fitness. You should give it a try someday," he said.

"Yeah, maybe. Maybe I will have desires soon."

"The other benefits of the fitness life are that your body will remain young, attractive. When you get old, you won't suffer a lot like most of the ordinary people do. You will be strong, robust, will be able to do lots of activities and not to get tired. But for that kind of life, you need a big commitment. I believe that any person can be committed with the right mindset," he told me with enthusiasm. I kept nodding and paying attention to what he was telling me without saying any words. My butt got soaked with wetness, I got up to give some air. He chuckled, saying.

"Too hot, huh."

"Yeah, it is. I am new here, still getting used to the environment," I explained to him by sitting back.

"Gotchu."

"So how long have you been living here? And how's life for you here? Are you married? Do you have kids? Sorry for asking too many questions at once."

"It's alright, good questions. I will answer them one by one," he said. He then started answering each question in detail. "I have been living here for 10 years." Before he continued, I gave a comment.

"Wow, a decade. It's been a while," I said with an impression.

"Yeah, indeed. I have been coaching for more than a decade. Originally, I graduated from the University with an IT degree. While studying my course, I joined one of my friends, who has been working out since he was 12. Day by day, I fell in love with fitness. I even had thoughts to drop out and pursue my professional fitness coaching career. But my parents encouraged me to finish my degree; they didn't mind me becoming a professional coach. They told me that someday, I would need my degree, on a rainy day, because who knows what to expect from life."

I asked him, "How old are you, by the way?"

"I am 35 now."

"So, you moved here in 2005?"

"Correct! I got the job here via an online application. Thanks to my close friend, I made an outstanding resume; even though being that young, it caught their attention. I had an online interview. But of course, before submitting my resume, I had to get my certificate. During my summer holidays out of my University, I did my best to improve my qualities, getting more and more experienced."

"So what gym are you currently working for?" I asked.

"Fitness First."

"Oh, I heard about it. It's a big international fitness brand. As far as my knowledge goes, they have lots of branches in the U.A.E. itself, not to mention other countries as well."

"Yes, you are right."

We had a pause. "Hey, let's walk while I answer your other questions," he said.

"Good idea," I said, supporting him.

We got up from the grass. My shorts soaked up. I felt better, my butt got some air, and my shorts started to slowly dry up. We started walking, and he kept on answering my questions. "Okay, to your second question. Life is really good here; I love it. Peaceful, safe, modern technologies, modern lifestyle. Everything is new here, literally," he said the last sentence with a louder enthusiastic voice.

"True, I agree with you," I responded to his information.

He continued, "You know, one thing I do not like here: the weather! It is so damn hot, especially in summer. You feel like you can't even breathe out of this high humidity. When I first arrived here, got off the airplane, boom, I wanted to get back on a plane, ha ha. The interiors are quite cool, no complaints about it. Most of the people are nice. I will repeat it again; it is really safe here, I can give it 5 stars for that. No crime. Nobody can hurt you, not even verbally. I heard that one man verbally cursed the other man on social media. He almost went into prison because of that but ended up paying a huge fine. Man, that is harsh. But it's good, you know, knowing the laws; no one can harm you at all," he ended his sentence, while I kept nodding and sipping my water, killing my frequent thirstiness. He sighed, smiled, and said.

"Ah, life is good here, life is good."

I smiled back at him. We walked in silence as if both of us were lost in our thoughts. However, I kept thinking of Ratanaporn; I talked to her on a video call a few days ago. The lights of the buildings kept flickering beautifully. We reached the walkway, which was near the water area of J.L.T., surrounded by tall buildings. There were also chairs a few meters away from the water's side. "Let's go and sit a little bit. I'll answer your third question," he suggested to me.

"Yeah, sounds good," I said.

We sat on one of the chairs.

"Okay. Can you repeat your third question again?" he asked me, forgetting about it.

"Yeah, no problem. Hmm, what was that..." For a moment, I forgot it myself, then it popped into my head. "Oh yeah, ah ha. Have you ever been married?"

"Nope! But most of my friends have been, in fact. Let me tell you something about being married. Marriage is a suicide." He paused.

I was startled by his statement. "Oh. Why is that?" I asked with a surprised reaction.

"You see, as soon as you get married, your freedom is over, personal life is over. Although I have never been married myself, nevertheless my friends have been. Hearing their experiences, I completely lost my desire for getting married on this short life of ours."

"Can you tell me in more details about their issues? I believe I would need to hear some stories, experiences about married life while still being young."

"Hmm, yeah, no problem," he narrowed his eyes looking at the buildings, then continued telling me more.

"When you get married, the first thing is that you will have big responsibilities such as paying bills, paying for rent, paying for trips, etc. On the other side, if a female partner works as well, it will be easier. If you want to have kids, you will even have to have stricter responsibility for your kids, of course, if you want to be a good parent. You need to make emotional, rational, and time investments for your marriage. As I said earlier, you will lose your freedom. You will be restricted to have funs. Less drinking, less partying, etc. Overall, you must be committed until the day you die. If you are not able to do any of those things, the divorce will start hunting you down. Your marriage will be broken, over. The worst part of marriage is the aftermath. If you got married to the wrong person, phew, good luck. During the divorcing process, you will have to give at least 50% of your wealth. It could be a house, a car, some amounts of money, and so on. Here is the worst part of what happened to my friends. One of my American friends who got divorced a few years ago, he ended up paying for child support, half of his wealth, his house was given to his ex-wife and two kids. On top of all that, the judge decided that he wouldn't be allowed to see his kids until they hit 18+. The system is really gonna drain the crap out of you, especially in the West. The judge gave him a note that if he fails to meet any of his orders, he would be in jail. To my mind, he is a good guy. He has always been nice to me, but the thing is, he never got to tell me the reasons for his divorce. Based on his situation, I can't give any comments about it. The other two scenarios are from my Kabayan friends. Their wives divorced them because, according to their reasons, my friends were too clingy for their wives. Luckily, neither of them had kids by the time of their separations. Their wealth has been sucked up from them too. In addition, had deep emotional damages. I know, it doesn't happen to all the couples, but having this kind of environment, having friends with such stories, until now, I don't want any marriage. Not even close to thinking about it. I guess these stories make some sense for you," he finished telling me.

People were passing by; some were just walking. I saw a few Caucasians and Arabs running around and passing by. Some were just standing, gazing at the water.

"Thank you for sharing. I will take it as consideration. These stories might help me to figure out something about my future," I responded to him. He just nodded.

Without noticing it, I realized that the time was close to midnight. My dad called me to return home immediately. As metro stations were already shut down, he told me to take a cab. When I finished talking to my dad, Randy asked me who I talked to. "I guess that is your parent?"

"Yeah, you are right. My dad got worried a little bit and told me to be back home now. Since all the metro stations are closed now, I will take a cab," I explained to him.

"I've got the car. I can drop you off at your place," he said.

"Oh really?"

"Yeah, sure," he replied with assurance. He smiled, and we headed to the parking. The streets were getting empty. I gazed up at the sky; a half-moon had shown its bright orange color. As I kept walking on Randy's left side, I gave no reaction to that kind of color.

We reached the parking lot. He had a Japanese car named Nissan 370Z. The car was white, including a red dragon's tune on the door from my side. It had a pedestal-designed spoiler attached to the back of the car, dyed in white as well. The windows were tinted in a deep black color; because of that, I was not able to have a look at the interior before getting in. It's from the Z generation of Nissan's sports cars. That one was Z34; prior to that, they produced Nissan 350Z, which was Z33. Z series of the Nissan's sports cars became famous worldwide thanks to the action movie… I really forgot the title of the movie.

"Awesome car," I said, observing it.

"Thanks, bud. I am fond of Japanese cars, especially Nissan Z series and Toyota Supra. Now, hop in," he said, unlocking the doors of his car. The seats' designs were black leather. As I sat on the seat, it was neither soft nor harsh, just a casual seat of the car. If drive for the long road, the butt will start to hurt and sweat badly.

We shut the doors, and he turned on the air conditioner. The air blew on my face, feeling so refreshing after walking in that hot weather. The steering wheel looked kind of expensive; I assumed he always took good care of his vehicle.

"Where do you stay?" he asked about my location.

"Dubai Marina. You can just drop me near the Dubai Marina metro station. Next, I'll just walk a few minutes to reach my building," I responded, telling him about my place.

"Alright, gotchu," he said.

He started the engine. Vroom, vroom, the car made a loud noise. I got curious when I heard such a loud engine sound. "Does this kind of car always have a loud engine noise?"

"Actually, the stock edition of Z series doesn't make a loud noise until you push to the limits. But for the Nismo editions, plus going to a mechanic and making minor changes, you can make your car as beastly as it is now. In addition, it doesn't cost much money," he explained to me with passion in his voice.

"Understood," I said. The car slowly moved from the parking and headed to the main road toward my location.

"Hey, do you like to listen to Hip-Hop music?" he asked while leaving the parking lot.

"Yeah, I like to listen to music. I listen to Hip-Hop from time to time."

"Awesome, now check this out," he replied by pressing the button that commanded the car to play songs. The beat sounded familiar to me. Boom boom, boom boom. Before the rapper began rapping the lyrics of the song, I guessed the song correctly.

"It is 50 Cent, In Da Club, right?" I asked Randy.

"Indeed, it is. Do you like this song?"

"Oh yeah. I used to listen to it often when I was a kid. I haven't tuned in for ages. Now you brought back my childhood memories," I told him, enjoying the song.

"Hey, Daler, how have you been feeling after the first session?" he asked me with a caring tone.

"Really fatigued; my whole body is in pain," I replied, with muscle pains.

"Don't worry, the more you train, the easier it will be for you. We are gonna do a push day for today. The muscles that we will work out for you today are chest, triceps and shoulders. Now go to the treadmill, warm up a little bit, then we will commence the session," he told me. I did as he said.

As a result of becoming friends with Randy, he somehow convinced me to join his gym. I agreed, worked out for a few weeks, and then gave up. Exhaustion began eating me up, and I wasn't able to catch up with my assignments. I complained a lot, and my dad told me to better stop if I didn't have the will to do it. Eventually, I realized that I didn't want that anymore. In spite of all that, Randy started to text me even more often, trying his best to persuade me to go back to gym.

Once I had stopped, I began to receive even more texts from him—work out motivational videos, quotes, even his own photos with his shredded body. Those were admirable, of course, but I realized that it wasn't my thing.

"Randy, bro, I really appreciate all these things and texts that you've been sending… no matter how hard I tried to get motivation from everything I have received from you, I am not being able to continue my workout. I won't lie and bring excuses to you; I will be honest, I just don't want it anymore…" I finally replied to his texts. The next day he saw my text.

"Too bad, man… I hope someday, you will have that fire in you, and will be back to the gym. Keep in touch, lil' bro." He replied. I simply sent him thumbs up and crossed fingers emojis.

Weeks

It happened in the early **weeks** of my dad and me moving to Dubai. That evening, I didn't go anywhere. We had a dinner chat. Since there were tons of different choices of meals to order online, my dad decided to stick with our traditional meals. He ordered two meals of manti, a type of Central Asian dumplings. The dining room was cool and chilly. At that time, I was still trying to adjust to living in a new place. My dad didn't seem to suffer any kinds of adaption. I guess, thanks to his early youth travels in most of the Asian countries, his immune system adapted very quickly to the new environment. He used to play Ping Pong, participating in International Tournaments. That is how he visited lots of new places. But as soon as he graduated from his university with a Financial Degree, he got a job and worked for a few years. He made friends with some businessmen who later became his partners in his Real Estate business. The business grew well gradually, and thanks to that, he was able to pay for all of our tuition fees for studying abroad, including providing us with a good life during our childhood, teenage years, and until we all graduated and found jobs. After ordering the dinner, he went to take a bath, meanwhile, I was preparing the table for the dinner.

The dinner had arrived; the door rang, I opened the door, and a tall, thin guy asked for my dad's name for confirmation.

"For Olim?"

"Yes," I replied. He handed me the bag with meals.

"Thank you for the order," he said and left. I thanked him back, locked the door, and took the meals to the dining room. The meals looked pretty fresh and smelled yummy. I opened both meal boxes and placed them on our plates. "All systems go," I muttered to myself.

By the time everything was ready, my dad came back from the bathroom wearing a plain white t-shirt with shorts and slippers. The table wasn't that big, but there were four chairs placed around it. He sat across from me. As in my homeland's culture, elders ate first, then the youth followed. In this case, my dad started first, and then me. I am pretty certain that most countries share a similar culture of elders eating first, but who knows? I haven't done much research about foreign countries up until the present moment. We ate in silence for a couple of minutes. I turned my head to the window's view while chewing my fresh tasty meal. The water was dark, with different sizes of yachts on its surface. I wondered to myself if sea animals slept at night as well. I wondered what would happen if someone falls into that oceanic water. Could killer whales or sharks bite you, or in the worst case, tear you down and eat you in that deep, dark, scary night marine water? As far as I knew, there were no reports about sharks or any marine animals in Dubai. People could swim with no worries, even swimming to the deeper side of the beach's ocean. Having those thoughts, my mind pondered over scenarios like what would happen if I swam at night alone or accidentally fell into that dark water. I wondered what it would feel like to be torn down into pieces, screaming out in horrible pain. The bones of my body would crack, and blood would spill all over the water. In sheer panic, a person wouldn't even see how their flesh was being broken down and eaten mercilessly. Does a person feel fear in those kinds of situations? Would one faint or just scream helplessly? Probably dragged down, which wouldn't even allow for screaming. Organs would be filled with the salted liquid of that water, and opening the mouth would allow it to fill up even quicker. What if one were just swallowed by a blue whale? The inside of each living habitat's creature on this planet Earth is full of darkness. Is a blue whale's interior filled with water? Would a person survive if swallowed by that giant sea animal? Only God knows what would happen. Can lifeguards save you from those awful occurrences in the water? What would it feel like to die in such situations? All these disturbing thoughts filled my mind during that short period of time. I glanced down at my table to have a glass of water. I sipped the water, which helped me push the meal down from my throat to my stomach. I took another bite of my second piece of manti. The second one had already cooled a bit, but the flavor didn't change. I munched with pleasure, filling up my half-hungry stomach. I took the second bite, chewed it well, and it floated deep into my stomach passively. The second piece was finished. While taking a bite of the third piece of my manti, out of the blue, my dad spoke up.

"Daler, son. You are growing up. Time flies fast. In a few years, you will be in your early 20s."

"Yes, dad, I know," I said with firmness.

"Good! You will be at the stage of that particular age's periods, where you will have to get married, have big responsibilities, and start your own family. Continuing our bloodline, making me and your mom loving grandparents," he told me with a commanding tone of voice, pointing at me with his fork.

I felt burdened hearing those words. On top of all, my parents never knew that I kept talking and having a pre-serious relationship with the Thai girl in the distance, hoping to meet her one day. I didn't want to continue that kind of topic. I just nodded in response. He munched his manti, then kept speaking. "I'll be having business trips starting from next year. Most of my trips will take place during the summer seasons. By the time I have enough finances in our budget, your mom and sisters will move in with us. I will bring them here as well." I kept eating my manti, only nodding to everything he told me. "You will be on your own during the times I will be out of Dubai. You must learn and get used to cleaning the apartment, doing all the chores, maybe even cooking some easy-made meals. Will you behave and won't make any troubles at those times?" he asked me with concern.

"Yes, I will, father. I will do my best to cope with everything on my own," I said in response.

"Very good. And don't worry, I will be leaving you enough amounts of money."

"Good to hear that," I replied with relief.

His phone rang. He checked the phone. "It's one of my partners. I guess it's an important call. You keep eating and finish. I will take care of the dishes when I am done talking on the phone. Just make sure to put your plate and glass in the sink," he told me and then left for his room to talk on the phone. When he told me that I would be left alone, I felt a great sense of relief. Nobody would tell me what to do; I would be able to do anything I wanted to. Deep inside me, I felt a freedom like I had never felt before. Frankly speaking, I loved that feeling.

I placed my dishes in the sink and went to the bathroom. I got naked and stared at my beardless face. Despite being 18 at that time, I didn't have a single hair of beard on my face. Strangely, the hair grew excessively on my armpits and pubes. I couldn't fathom if it was because of my genes or not. I was ashamed to talk about such topics with elders in my family. It made me distressed to even think about talking it with them.

I made up my mind to fill up the bathtub with hot water to relax a little bit. I took the tub stopper, inserted it into the hole of the tub, twisted to the hot side, and then it passively started to fill up with warm water. Meanwhile, I heard my dad talking loudly on the phone but didn't bother to listen carefully to what he was talking about. My whole attention was towards the flowing hot water from the tub's spout. The steam was emerging from the flow.

At last, the bathtub had filled with warm water. I slowly immersed myself in it. My whole body felt relaxed. I dived my head, brought it out, and almost all the pain was alleviated from my mind. I leaned my head on the surface of the tub's end and made a deep sigh. I recalled when Ratanaporn left me on seen for the second time in a row in the past. Although I felt hurt when I was left on seen for the first time, the second time didn't hurt me that much. I remained positive that she would text me back.

My patience paid off. That time, it didn't take her much time to reply. She replied a week later, again with a reason. My mind was vague about that particular reason. No matter how hard I tried to recall it, nothing popped into my head. I gave up eventually. By default, my mind started thinking about my father telling me about getting married. It really didn't make sense to me. Maybe it would make sense if I had never met Ratanaporn. At early ages, I had the same mentality as my peers, as elders in my family, about getting an arranged marriage right after graduating from my university. Thanks to Ratanaporn, my mentality had changed; I envisioned a different kind of lifestyle. It never crossed my mind to get married with Ratanaporn, but I foresaw a long-term relationship with her, despite being far away from each other. 'Where there is real love, the distance would never matter,' I always kept that motto. It made me wonder if she thought the same way. Even if she didn't, I imagined myself conquering her heart at any cost. That's how strong my love had been for her.

My dad called me all of a sudden. He asked me what I was doing in the bathroom for over one hour. I had a flow of thoughts that made time fly fast like a rocket. I let the water down, turned the shower on, cleaned myself well, wiped my entire body slowly, put on my t-shirt and underwear, then left the bathroom heading straight to my room. The light in the dining room was already switched off, and my dad was already in his room. I had nothing else to say to my dad. I opened my bed's blanket, jumped on my bed, and laid down with my head gazing at the ceiling. I made up my mind to text Ratanaporn and share the news about my dad's trips.

"I assume it is late morning over there now. So, good morning to you. Hope you are doing well. I have important news to share with you. My dad spoke to me earlier during dinner. He told me that he would go on business trips starting from next year, especially more often in summers. We have been texting and caring for each other for years, I can say three years already." I thought about coming clean about my love for her, but something deep inside me held me back from it. As much as we spent time together virtually from afar, I felt that she felt some affections for me as well, but she didn't confess to me either. Maybe she felt the same way I felt, I don't know. Then, I went on. *"Here is the benefit for us about my dad's trips. We will have a great opportunity to meet in real. We can make plans and save some amounts of money. You can visit me here in Dubai and stay at my place, which would cut lots of costs. From my point of view, this is a good idea. We must meet at some point in real. We have to do everything in our power to make that happen. I will be waiting for your reply to this. Sending a big hug."* I ended the text. The text showed delivered. Without any worries, I turned the Wi-Fi off, expecting to see her reply by the time I wake up.

It was a weekend; I woke up late in the afternoon. Usually, I awakened feeling hungry, but that afternoon, I felt like my stomach was full. When I checked the apartment, I didn't see my dad's presence. I did my ordinary routine: took a piss, washing my face, my teeth, and headed to the kitchen to make some coffee. The kitchen and dining room were pretty connected; the only thing that kept them separate was the small wall and upper long bar narrow table. On the down part of the table, I was heating the water on a water heater for my coffee. We did have the coffee maker, but I was indolent to make coffee on that machine, so instead, I made the three-in-one coffee. The water got heated, I opened the small package of the coffee, put it in my mug, poured the water, and slowly started mixing it up. I never added sugar to it because it already tasted sweet enough and had some sugar in the ingredients. I sat down on one of the chairs which directed with the window view. I passively began drinking a hot three-in-one coffee.

Later on, I received a positive text from Ratanaporn about meeting in person.

"Dearest Daler. I have read your text. I am touched right now. I feel the same way. We must definitely meet in person. We have been spending time together virtually for a while. Yes, this is the best idea. I hope we will meet one day (praying emoji). Of course, I want to make the plan about it with you as well. I will wait for that moment for you to inform me about that news.

"I had a tiring and busy day. I know you always understood me about such matters. I am going to sleep now. Enjoy your daytime. Chat you later!"

Reading that text brought a smile to my face, making my mood brighter. Someday, I always believed that I would confess my love for her. I was thinking of doing it when we would meet in person.

Months had passed. That next year's summer, my dad did what he told me he would do, but a bit differently. He left in the middle of spring for his business trips to some Russian cities, including my homeland, telling me that he had plans to bring the family by that year's summer. Something changed, and he returned to Dubai by the end of spring. So, my plan to meet Ratanaporn in Dubai fell off as well. I tried to ask him the reasons why his plans changed. He gave me a short answer with a scowled face. "Plans changed."

I asked him with hints to get a better answer with more details, but to no avail; I got the same response. Eventually, I gave in and stopped asking him about the reasons.

At the end of the day, my dad realized his plans. That year passed, and in one year, he left Dubai for my homeland to prepare the documents to bring them to Dubai. He stayed in my homeland for the whole summer. That year, he didn't only fly to my country; he was out of Dubai most of the time. I lived alone, being free.

Semester

After that special night with Ju, my perception and my vision had changed. I gained some sort of confidence. Mentally, I felt like a grown-up man. Strangely, when weeks passed, I noticed facial hair growth. I saw tiny, thin hair above my lip seeding up, and some thin side beards, and under my lower lip too. In general, serious maturity hit me up. She taught me lots of things about relationships, sex, and all those sorts of advices about being with a girl. What can I call the times I had spent with her? I can't call it an official relationship because neither of us strived for it. Friends with benefits? I don't think I can refer to that either. To my mind, friends with benefits only sleep with each other, having a good time. I think the right way to call it is my mentor for girls because I lost my virginity with her. The night will forever be in my mind; I can never erase it. I don't repent as well. It all seemed natural to me, like it was supposed to be that way. It was my life's fate. I lied to my dad that I made new Chinese male friends. Thanks to all my lies, I could visit her 4–5 times a week. I always told my dad that my Chinese friends loved to play games and invited me to join them. In addition, I told him that they were juniors and helped me to study for my courses. Once he asked me to show their photos. Little did I know that Ju was an excellent editor? She edited my photo with her own friends beside me, then sent the photo to me. It astonished me to see her skills; it looked so real, with me smiling and standing beside three Chinese male guys at the indoor campus of my university. When I showed the photo on my phone, it sufficed to convince him, and he never questioned me again about that. This is how I got away from any arguments, fights with my dad, and my family. We passed our project successfully. Despite passing it, it didn't go smoothly. A week before the project's due date, she and those two Indian girls had a dispute. They argued in the middle of the group's meeting. The Indian girls considered her lazy, not helping enough to pass our project. Not to take anyone's side, but in my eyes, she did enough for us to receive passing grades. Those Indian girls were not willing to get just the passing grades; they wanted the highest in the group. Perhaps that was one of the reasons that they gave Ju bad feedback. They didn't talk to me much, maybe because I was the youngest, and they didn't take me seriously. The funny thing was that when both sides ran out of English vocabulary, their native words kept coming out of their mouths. I couldn't do anything except watch. In the end, they exhausted each other and left the room. First, the Indian girls left the group meeting room, then in a few minutes, me and Ju left as well. By our last meeting, Indian girls cooled off, and we presented our project. As a result of that little drama, I came to understand why adults complained about working with different people. One fails to meet others' expectations and vice versa. Thankfully, I passed all my subjects and finished my first freshman

semester. The University gave students two weeks break upon the next spring session.

During that break, I hung out with Ju every single day. On each hangout, I had sex with her. I can say I had a sex marathon. Those were the best two weeks of my entire young adult years. The best part was that her dad was out of Dubai, nobody disturbed us. She didn't even invite her friends over when hanging out with me. Only two of us enjoyed our times at our best.

The spring session commenced. The weather was at its best time—cool, little wind, wearing jackets, jeans, even winter hats, etc. No air conditioning was needed. We kept hanging out for three more weeks of that semester.

One day, on a Wednesday afternoon, she didn't attend the class. I texted her; she saw my text but no reply. I texted her again, asking if everything was alright with her. The same thing happened again—left on seen. I stopped messaging her until the weekend. I messaged her for the third time on Sunday evening, and the text wasn't delivered, showing that her internet was off. I called her; the number wouldn't be available. I tried to reach her with different methods.

By Monday, I talked to one of our professors about her. Sadly, when I mentioned her name, the professor either changed the topic or completely ignored my questions about her. I had gone that far to get the information from our dean. It took me a few days to meet him in his office personally. I can't recall the precise day of the appointment he gave me; I guess it took place by the end of that same week. I went to his office before evening time. I knocked on his door a few times then pushed it slowly towards his office. I greeted him while still pushing the door.

"Good day, Mr. Kumar. May I enter?" I asked politely. He nodded and greeted me back.

"Good day, Daler."

"First of all, thank you for your time."

"No issues. What can I help you with?"

"Ahh," I paused for a second, considering how to explain our relationship. I chose the easiest way.

"One of my friends from the campus has been gone. I tried to reach her, but her phone has been off, and her number as well. I came here to ask you if you know the reasons for why she disappeared all of a sudden. I would really appreciate your help regarding this issue. She has been my closest friend from our university."

"Hm, alright. Provide me her full name. I will search her in our system."

Little did I realize that I never knew her full name? It never crossed my mind to ask her full name.

"Her name is Ju. Unfortunately, I can't recollect her surname," I told him with hesitation.

"In that case. dear Daler, I can't help you. You have to provide me the full name of the student. If she were your real best friend, you would know her full name. Now, you must leave; I have work to do."

I was out of words, filled with shame from his response. "Thank you for your time again," I replied to him with an awful reaction deep inside me. He smiled, and I left his office room. His bitter judgement about best friends was right on the spot; I couldn't agree more with that, nevertheless, I got hurt.

I accepted the true reality that Ju had been irretrievable lost from my life, from my world. A sense of regret poured down on my soul for not asking her full name or inquiring about her social media accounts. I went to my afternoon class with a hurt and lost soul.

For a few weeks, I lived my life in misery. I remembered that she told me she might leave Dubai for a new country as she was bored. The other thing I remembered her saying after spending weeks with her was.

"If I decide to leave someday, for sure I will let you know." She told me that in the middle of having our shots. Although we were already tipsy, nevertheless, I had believed her words, as she never broke them during our hangouts. Whatever she told me, she did it with no doubts. Therefore, I couldn't be dubious about her words.

Remarkably, she had vanished from my thoughts at the end of that semester. I had started dating a new Asian girl who was Chinese too. We first saw each other in a food court. The place was crowded, and she sat right next to me. I didn't bother talking to her that day. We bumped into each other, making slight eye contacts and smiling. Thanks to all of my experiences with Ju, I had got the courage to say hi to her following our last encounter before beginning to socialize with her more frequently.

Unlike Ju, she was tall, around five feet and eight inches, almost my height. I was just a few centimeters taller than her. She had a slim rectangle body shape. She wore old-fashioned rounded glasses with a mini skirt and a shirt and some sneakers. That was her outfit most of the time. I can say that, every time I saw her, her legs glowed from cleanliness. I couldn't help but look back just to have a look at her legs after each of our encounters. The day I bumped into her, greeting her and continuing the conversation, she was wearing a white off-shoulder shirt with a black mini skirt and some branded shoes that I didn't recognize. Anytime we passed by, she always had a book in her hands.

"Don't ever try to give those lame, stupid pick-up lines when you first want to talk to a girl," Ju once told me.

"Hey. How are you? No books today?" I asked her in the middle of the walkway to the food court. She stopped; it took her seconds to respond to me.

"Ah… Hello. I am good, thanks. Yeah, I left my books at the library this time," she greeted me back, explaining about her books.

"That makes sense," I said. We awkwardly kept silence.

As she was trying to leave my side, I decided to break the silence. "You are going to eat right now, correct?"

"Um, yes."

"Do you mind if I join you? I am getting hungry myself," I told her, feeling nervous inside, fearing to be rejected.

Luckily, she agreed. "Umm, okay," she replied.

"Great, let's head there."

Then we walked to the food court. The sky gradually gave way to dusk. I wasn't actually hungry, as I was heading back to the campus from the food court itself. I had to say something to her to spend more time with her. I guess she was surprised when I asked her to join. I suppose she didn't want to be rude by rejecting me. What a sweetheart.

The food court wasn't crowded when we entered it. I decided to order something light with a soft drink. I ordered chickened chicken twister with a soda. Seeing her shape, nobody would say that she ate a lot. She made a large order, having 4 crispy chickens, a medium chicken sandwich, large spicy fries, and a large soda. I insisted on paying for her meal, but she refused, saying.

"No, no, no. Sorry, I will pay for myself now. Maybe someday." Hearing that ached my heart. However, the last line gave me hope. It took me a couple of minutes for our orders to be ready. Expecting a different thing, they gave us our orders on one tray. I smiled and told her that I would take the tray. She smiled back and didn't mind that. I took our tray, and we searched for seats. Even though there were a few people there, we explored the whole food court, eventually deciding to sit in the corner at a small table with just two seats. Half of the people eating their meals were employees of the food court. The lights with shadows covered the outdoors. I saw through the glassed walls of the food court students leaving campuses. There were times that I stayed until 9 P.M. to 11 P.M. at the library, preparing for my quizzes or serious tests. Usually, the majority of the students left the campus between 5 P.M. to 7 P.M.

The time showed 6:30 P.M. on the clock which hung on the left side of the food court's wall. No wonder why the numbers of crowded students were leaving when I had a look through that window wall that we were heading to sit and eat our meals.

We sat across from each other. Only a few people's voices speaking in their languages were heard, so we didn't have to speak loudly as in crowded times. As my stomach was full with one medium pizza about 30–40 minutes ago, I took small bites out of my twister sandwich. Compared to me, she started eating big.

"What is your name, by the way?" I asked her, swallowing my food.

"My name is Hui Xiang. What about you?" She told me and asked me, mixing her spicy fries with ketchup.

"I am Daler," I responded. "Hu… Hushing…? I am sorry, can you repeat one more time? It is the first time I hear such a name. It sounds beautiful but hard to pronounce for my language."

She chuckled. "Just call me Xiang. Okay? This way, it won't be hard to remember."

"Xiang! Got you," I said, repeating her name after her.

We kept munching our meals. "So, are you new here?" I asked.

She looked straight into my eyes. "No, this is my pre-last semester. The short summer semester will be my final," she told me, then began consuming her soft drink through the metallic straw.

"Mm, you are a senior, that's amazing. I am still considered a freshman. This has been my only second semester." She nodded with a smile to what I told her without any response. I thought about what else to ask her. "What is your course?"

"I had been doing BCOM, Accounting," she replied.

"Ah, I see. Has it been difficult in accounting?" I followed up with corny questions just not to be in an awkward silence. Meanwhile, I barely swallowed my twister sandwich, drinking after each bite to push it down into my stomach.

"Not really," she said, giving me a short answer. No matter how hard I tried to keep the conversation going, I ran out of topics. She didn't ask me anything either. We ended up finishing our meals without a word, only hearing other people's foreign voices in our surroundings. We stood up. I dared to ask her for her mobile number because I didn't want to let her go, hoping to give myself a new chance with Ju's disappearance.

"Can I get your mobile number? I enjoyed our conversation." She hesitated, and looked around.

"Umm, okay." I got her number, saved it on my contact list, willing to make further calls. We exited the food court in silence again, parting with just saying goodbyes.

I hadn't seen her since the completion of that spring semester. I called her, only empty dial tones transcended into my ears. One week passed; I called her several times, and nothing happened again. I had no choice but to be patient in that situation. Three weeks passed; I called her, and at last, she picked up my call.

"Hello, Xiang. How have you been?" I greeted her.

"Hello… Who is this?"

I paused, surprised why she had forgotten about me so quickly. "This is Daler calling you…"

"Who is Daler? I don't remember anyone by that name, sorry."

I felt embarrassed; my throat dried up. I had no idea what to say. Then I made my last attempt. "We had dinner in the food court a few weeks ago before the end of our semester. We bought some fast food. In addition, prior to having that dinner, we bumped into each other from time to time…"

I sighed to myself. She listened carefully, giving herself time to recall. "Hmmm… oh yes, now I remember. You are that Asian-looking guy, a freshman."

"Yes, that is correct," I replied to her with relief.

"I saw this number called me numerous times. I don't pick up strangers' numbers. I got exhausted and gave it a shot to pick it up."

"Yeah, I called you many times. Actually, it is my own fault. I had to give you at least a missed call after our dinner for you to save my number, sorry for that."

I heard a chuckle from her line. "It's alright."

"Let's hang out, have dinner, walk on the beach…? Also, we could know more about each other as well. So, what do you say?" I asked her anxiously.

"Umm, okay, that sounds interesting. What place would you suggest?"

"Dubai Marina Mall, we can grab dinner there. And JBR is close to that place as well."

"We can just stay in the mall. It is hot now. Don't you think we will melt down while walking?"

"That makes sense. Are you okay on Friday evening of this week, at 6 P.M.?"

"Fridays' evenings are always crowded. Let's do it on Saturday, same time, 6 P.M.," she told me, proposing a new plan.

"Yes indeed, didn't think about that. Alright, Saturday it is then."

"Good! By the way, I will save your number now, ha ha," she said with a cheerful voice.

"Ha ha, yeah, that would be good," I replied.

"Okay, see you soon!"

"See you!" We hung up, the call ended.

Starting from that year's summer, my feelings grew more and more to Ratanaporn. We chatted, made video calls every single day with set schedules according to our times. I felt more in love with her. Those kinds of feelings made me not to want to lose her ever, at any cost. Yet, I wasn't able to tell her how much my love grew for her, stronger and stronger. On her side, she didn't come clean either. The other thing was that I wasn't alone in that situation. My heart lightened from the burden of responsibilities. Nevertheless, we knew deep down in our hearts that we had been fond of each other. The shyness, the insecurities prevented us from confessing to each other. A ray of hope in my heart kept me positive, that I would surely meet her in real. I believed she had hopes for the same cause.

The day had arrived. I began preparing myself for the date with Xiang. First, I took a cold shower which helped me to wake up my slow blood circulation from my late sleep a day before the date's day. I finished showering with fresh feelings in my whole body, including mentally. I wiped myself up, dried my long undercut hairstyle. I went to my closet to put a new underwear, and returned to the bathroom to shave my thin beard. I looked at myself in the mirror proudly, finally having a beard. I kept staring at my face. Indeed, I looked like an Asian person. I had slightly monolid eyes. No wonder why. According to my knowledge of what I had learned from school history about my country, my culture, lots of wars took place within more than 2,000 years since the Eastern Persians inhabited Central Asia. The first war took place against Alexander the Great during his war conquests. The second war occurred against Arabic Khalifats. The third happened against Mongols, Genghis Khan's war conquests. The last and most recent was against Soviet's Bolsheviks, Russians. As a result of all these wars, people had gotten mixed up. Based on my Asian looks, I assumed around 70% of my DNA could be from Mongolians, who are Asians. I stopped my vigorous stare at myself, passively put the shaving foam on my face, and then slowly began shaving my thin beard. It didn't take me long to be done shaving. I left the bathroom with thoughts of what to wear.

I arrived at the mall, wearing ripped gray jeans with a white oversized shirt and black sneakers. She called me right when I entered the mall.

"Hey! Where are you? I am here waiting near the entrance."

"Hi. Yeah, I am here, but I can't see you," I responded with a puzzle.

"I am standing on the right-side of a corner, having a ponytail, without my glasses," she directed me. I turned to my right side. I saw her having that black hair in a long ponytail style wearing a long-sleeved white blouse with a long skirt, and as usual sneakers. Her entire outfit was in white color. I approached her.

"Good evening, Xiang. Nice outfit; you just look like a high school girl from Japanese animes," I greeted her with a comment on her outfit.

"Hey, good evening. Yes, you could say so," she replied with a smile. "Do you like it, though?"

"Yes, it suits you well."

The mall was full of people walking in different directions with different styles. The cool interior atmosphere refreshed me even better. Next, I suggested where we can eat our dinner.

"There are some restaurants behind the mall's exit. We can eat there. We should go down to the last floor for the exit."

"Hmm, yeah, I know one of those, have seen them in the past, but I never tried to eat there," she responded.

"That's good. Me neither, gonna be a new experience for those restaurants for us," I said cheerfully.

She nodded and smiled. While walking side by side, headed to the escalators to go down, I grabbed her left hand. Her soft thin hand was a bit wet. I assumed she had to walk for a few minutes to enter the mall. That evening's humid hot weather sweated her pretty good. I myself dried up quickly. Maybe she was nervous or something. Whatever caused her palms to sweat, I enjoyed and gained confidence holding it.

We exited the mall. There were restaurants on either sides. Each restaurant had seats outdoors as well as indoors. We decided to head for the left one.

There weren't many people sitting outdoors. Some were just chilling, smoking shishas. The waiter greeted and took us indoors. It was a typical Arabic-designed restaurant. He showed us the available seats. As from our first dinner, we decided to sit in the corner again. The walls of the restaurant were glass-made. We could gaze at the skyscrapers from our seats. It had a light blue brightness. The table was kind of big, with two couched soft-designed chairs. We sat across from each other.

"What are your orders," the waiter asked us with a fatigued smile on his face.

"Do you have steaks?" I asked.

Meanwhile, Xiang was checking the menu.

"Yes, we do."

"Okay, that's good. I want a well-done steak with fries and a Coke." The waiter nodded and wrote my order down on his small order pad, then looked at her side. She finished checking the menu and ordered.

"I want fried salmon with rice and a Coke." He wrote her order down, then left our sides.

"You like Coke too?" I asked with curiosity.

"Yes, I do."

"Looks like we have something in common," I gave her a line. She just gave me a bored smile reaction. She spent her time texting rigorously fast to someone, didn't even flinch until the order arrived. I sat there completely perplexed, not a single word came out of my mouth.

At last, the waiter brought our orders. The smell of her fish filled up the air around our table. "Have a nice appetite," wished us a waiter and left our side.

She finished her texting. "I am so sorry for that. I really had to reply to those important texts."

"It's okay," I said with a low tone, being annoyed inside.

"Thank you for understanding. The meal looks tasty. Let's eat now," she said with a smile.

"Yeah," I replied while munching my steak. I asked who that was that she had been texting so focused.

"If you don't mind… Can you tell me who you had been texting with?" She chewed her fish, swallowed it, then looked into my eyes and responded.

"It was my mom. I asked her about my daughter's condition. She has been having a fever since yesterday. She is only 6. My mom assured me that I don't have to worry much; the doctor prescribed her some medicines. She is a little bit better now. I texted her 3 hours before our hangout, and she was able to reply just a moment ago. Therefore, I had to reply. Sorry again for this inconvenience. Being a mother can be worrisome," she told me her reasons and apologizing one more time. I puzzled when she said that she had a kid. Instantly, what came to my mind was to ask about her age.

"Wow, you have a kid. How old are you?"

"I am 29. Will be 30 soon this year."

"Ah, I see. It's sweet that you have a kid."

"Thank you."

"Are you married now?" I asked.

"No, I divorced 2 years ago. He cheated on me while I was here studying." After those words, she kept telling me all her years of the relationship with her ex-husband. How they fell in love in high school. How she worked hard in cosmetology to maintain their marriage finances. Although her relatives advised her to study abroad, she always refused by telling them that she had enjoyed her marriage, didn't need much. By the time they had a baby, they had to provide more for her family. She quitted cosmetology to learn English for studying abroad. Her uncle promised to pay for her and her husband for their tuition fees. No matter how many times she tried to convince her husband to join her, he rejected and preferred to stay in their motherland. She kept traveling during the semester breaks to maintain her marriage and to see her baby. She remained loyal to her husband while being distant. Despite all of that, her husband cheated on her openly without a shame, left her and their daughter. Thankfully, her mom decided to help her by taking care of her daughter until she returned to China. She had been in pain for some time. There was still a scar remaining in her heart. But thanks to her goals, she was able to overcome it. Frankly speaking, I felt bad for her after hearing her relationship story. On the other hand, it attracted me more into her.

A few weeks passed, and we got along together well. We got into a relationship, which was the first official relationship in my life. We went on many dates, and she even postponed her trip to China, expressing her growing fondness for me. After each time we had sex, she would begin sharing all the details about her past experiences with her husband. There were times when I grew tired of her stories, but I remembered Ju's advice.

"The key to successfully winning a girl is to show her your affections through emotions, to court her, and most importantly, it is all about listening to her attentively. Whatever happens, even if you feel exhausted listening to her, never ever forget to use this skill. Remember, listening, listening, listening!" The sincerity of our relationship was evident. However, I found it challenging to completely sever ties with Ratanaporn during my relationship with Xiang. I found ways to keep chatting or calling Ratanaporn behind the scenes. Can I be blamed for cheating? Maybe yes. Since we were not officially in a relationship with Ratanaporn, I remained calm, not burdened with guilt. All this led me to nothing but confusion, with mixed feelings about why these things were happening to me. Love is hard to understand, hard to perceive. Every person has their own definitions of being loved and loving someone. At that time, I happened to have a misguided perception of love that led me to these actions. Moreover, I was unable to fathom what was wrong and what was right for me; this was all new to me.

I spent repetitive days with her throughout the entire summer. We hung out, had sex, and I listened to her complaints. As much as I enjoyed my relationship with her, the consequences seemed inevitable. By the end of August, she called me to visit her apartment, telling me that it's urgent.

"You need to come now; we need to talk. My friends are not here now, so I am alone. No questions, please, just come."

"Okay," I responded, pondering about her urgency. She hung up the call, the line was deadly silent, and I hung up, sweating, worrying, and shivering a little bit. I dressed up quickly, rushed, left the apartment, and took a cab.

Her expressionless face opened the door. Speechless, she turned around and walked forward. Dumbfounded, I followed her with no other choices. I sensed negativity, and my throat dried up out of nervousness. The room was as tranquil as in a void of nothingness. We sat on the sofa; she sat beside me, head down, hands on her laps. She remained in that position… I can't recollect for how long it was, as I was completely paused, eyes wide open, staring at the TV's dark, lifeless screen a few feet away.

"Daler," her low tone of voice called me. I turned my head; her head was still down. "Daler!" she repeated and raised her head, turning it to my side. I said nothing.

"I am so sorry," she said with a gloomy face. "I am really sorry…" she apologized again, and the word "sorry" echoed in my ears.

"Why...? What's happened? I asked her, my heart rate elevated."

She looked straight into my eyes. "Before I explain everything in detail... promise me you will listen to me carefully, understand me well. Do you promise?"

I had no other answer but to agree. "Yes, I promise!" I said firmly.

She sighed, and then she began her explanations. "Ah, Daler. I really love you; I do. What we did together, how we spent time together, will forever be in my memories, in my heart," she said, placing her right hand on her small left breast. I was touched when she said that. She continued. "You even treated me better than my ex-husband; you are such a lovely young guy, such a caring person. You always listened to me; no other guy would do that. Even my ex-husband never listened to me carefully the way you did." She paused and glanced down on her lap again. The words hit my mind.

"Ju's wisdom helped me a lot. Thank you, Ju. I owe you a lot." She glanced up, gazed towards me, and sighed again. "Ah, all those sexual things we did, oh my God, I am so pleased and blessed that I had been able to enjoy them to the fullest. I allowed you to do those things that I never allowed any other man because I seriously always have been feeling free, comfortable around you. These are the main reasons that I am explaining these things to you." Hearing her words, I even wondered why she apologized before her explanations. Then the real deepest confessions hit me. I noticed small tear drops streaming down her face. I was startled, didn't know what to say or what actions to take. I let her continue the rest of her confessed explanations.

"You are so, so young. People say age doesn't matter in love, but in reality, it matters a lot. I don't want to get older than you much faster, die earlier than you. What we had was an emotional experience without thinking of our future. Moreover, I have a kid, I need a man to raise my kid with. I need a man to take responsibility to care for me, for my kid, for our future. I will not say you are an irresponsible guy. It's just… it will be hard for you to understand. Lastly, I will leave Dubai; I won't stay here and will never be back. I will work in my motherland, for some foreign company to make use of the courses I had done here. Daler, I hope you understand me. Please don't be sad." More tears streamed down her face. I said nothing and moved closer to her. We embraced each other for the last time.

I left her apartment, feeling sorrowed. I was overwhelmed by sadness after sadness. First Ju, then Xiang—back-to-back losses. The situations differed, of course. At least I knew of Xiang's departure.

Despite all of my relationships with those girls, despite feeling sadness and sorrow, I never regretted losing them. I never wanted them back. One girl had always been deep in my thoughts, deep in my heart—Ratanaporn.

Nature

I heard the loud drumbeats, "Duk duk, duk duk." It kept pulsating passively. I counted each beat unconsciously, like an automated robot made only for counting, "Four, five, six…" I reached the number sixty-six. Next, I started hearing heavy breaths, ins and outs out of my fragile flesh. Why had I experienced such weird sensations? Why do I still remember them? It was beyond the way I could comprehend the reasons. I sensed the shivering of my body on the wet sheet. I moved around my bed, yet not being able to open my eyes. I tried to open them, but my brain didn't respond. I strived for my second attempt, but with the fruitless result. The sense of touches came to my head, to my hands, to my legs, to my entire body. I unconsciously panicked, and my heart even started pounding faster, ready to explode. All I had in my mind was fear, horror, helpless being. The sense of that momentum seemed to continue for ages.

I opened my eyes in full pain. The light white dots flew around my vision. I tried to observe my surrounding, but the dots covered my vision. I winked, rubbed my eyes, hoping to restore my eyesight; it didn't work. Moments passed rapidly.

At long last, my body relaxed; the panic was gone. I saw a small lamp attached to the table, shinning the glim light. I noticed a chair beside the table. Not a single soul showed its presence. I realized I was sitting on a chair myself, back leaned on the post, arms hung over the chair. A transparent-walled room displayed on my left side. The room had a king bed in the center, painted completely in white. I had no reactions, zero emotions to the entire interior of where I seated. I decided to close my eyes, wishing it all would vanish from my sight. I closed my eyes for a few seconds, opened them back… A faceless man brought its appearance into my view. No words came out of my mouth. Dead quietness was the only matter that existed in that room. He had a hat on his head, a white shirt with a black tie under his black suit. He held a giant knife swirling in his left hand. I glanced down; nothing was visible downwards. I looked back at him. The vague thoughts struck my mind that I saw that man somewhere else. Despite my efforts trying to recollect whether or not my memories deceived me, I gave in. Out of the blue, Ratanaporn popped into my head. I recalled sleeping in one bed, spooning with her warm soft flesh. I fell asleep peacefully for the first time in my life. Neither emotional nor physical torments could prevail over that harmony of our hushed sleep. Meanwhile, the faceless man stopped swirling his knife. Legs crossed, wearing black pants, and black shoes. At that moment, the chance came to me; I saw his entire outfit. A low husky voice spoke up from that table. **"Daler, we know who you are. We know what are you. We have been watching you since you were born. We watch from the sky. We watch under the ground. We see everything in this universe in small** details. We have unmatched powers in this universe. We exist, yet human eyes cannot see us." He stopped; the sound of my heartbeat returned. I did my best to move my lips to say something in response, but he interrupted me. "You won't be able to speak at this moment. You will only be able to listen to me. I am here to preach, to convey to you an important lifetime message. Thus, pay careful attention to what I will inform you. This is a once-in-a-lifetime opportunity. We did this to each person on Earth, at the right time, in the right moment. Not everybody remembered our message; not everybody succeeded. Those who failed to learn a lesson from us are the people who are doomed, who will continue to live a miserable life until death. We know you are a clever, kind-hearted boy. We are certain you will remember my preach word by word. However, we know nobody is perfect. Therefore, I will repeat one more time. Take heed of each word that will be conveyed to you.

Throughout centuries of mankind's existence, humans have always had the highest dopamine, the highest erotic senses. None of the animals, from the tiniest to the largest, have the ability to control their sexual desire. They fight for mating, winners take it all, and losers lose it all. They either die for it or succeed for it. Humans have the highest intellect, the highest intelligence, the highest chance of being able to control their lust. In spite of these gifts, humans fail enormously to control these lusts. However, it can be said that these phenomena are part of human nature. Inversely, it is a lifetime test for humans, having such traits." A stone wall of silence surrounded me. I was still in the same position; nothing changed. He swirled his knife; his deep, husky, low voice came to life again. **"We guided you to that way on purpose. What I mean by that way is when you slept with two Chinese girls while loving Ratanaporn. You always sensed you two would eventually meet each other in real. Yet, you couldn't wait for that moment. On the other hand, she dated some boys too; I cannot tell you the numbers. Although she dated boys, she never kissed nor hugged those boys, not to mention sleeping with them. She always bore you deep in her heart. She patiently waited for that perfect moment. You see, we put both of you in a great test. You might think you failed big time. Indeed, you did. Do not worry, Daler. Do not let your spirit suffer. Do not be disheartened; just remember my words, remember them well!**

We always make sure people make the right choices after serious matters. We always guide them to the right, truthful path. Deep inside their hearts, they sense; they hear our guidance. People know if they act in a certain way, it will end up good for them. Despite that, their lust overcome them. On that occasion, we put them in a bad position, punish them with bad consequences.

Let me reveal you about fabrication. People love to lie to each other. People even lie to themselves. Sometimes it is useful to be untruthful, sometimes it is useless. If people kept telling the truth all the time, the truth would lose its value. You cannot literally do that, telling the truth to people all the time. This lying is one

of the spiritual aspects of humanity. Fabrication is an ally of the Universe. It helps to keep the balance. May this revelation be kept in your head for ages!

Now, for you to have a balanced life, I will give you an important piece of advice. It will be your choice whether or not to follow the advice. In advance, I will convey to you, we know she will never come clean to you about the guys she dated in the past. You are lucky if shares a little bit of information about that topic. We know how you and Ratanaporn feel for each other. If both of you confess, especially you, your relationship with her will be ruined for the rest of your life. My advice to you is to never ever confess to her about your affairs. It may sound unfair; it may sound harsh… Trust me, it is for your own good." With that being said, he stopped his speech. Again, he started swirling his sharp knife. The pure sound of my heartbeat came to life, and I began hearing each beat. Unlike earlier, the beat sounded slow, as if the entire event transformed into slow motion. I recalled the night's moments before going to sleep. We went back home after visiting downtown. We were getting slightly hungry on our way to my place. Upon reaching home, I wanted her to try our traditional meal, pilaf. There were a few restaurants serving that dish, so it wasn't that hard to find and order.

"Only if you agree to try Thai meals as well," she agreed, following my advice for eating my traditional meal first.

"Deal!" I replied quickly, winking at her. The dinner arrived just by the time we refreshed ourselves by taking a bath. She seemed to enjoy the food. We ate in silence, occasionally making eye contact and showing each other warm smiles. We felt fatigued, decided to go to bed right after finishing our meals. We jumped into the bed, got under the blanket, cuddled, and fell asleep.

Memories vanished; my consciousness got back to that dimly lit room with a faceless man. When I looked at him, his head was facing my direction. A weird creature, being on a human's flesh, being able to talk somehow, convey revelations for my own good, having unimaginable strongest powers… and yet, not having a face. Vagueness devoured my mind; I felt numbness in my entire body, I couldn't even sense my spirit, my own being; all seemed lost at that moment. The faceless man got up from his seat, stood up, his knife in his left hand, his head kept straight, and gazing at my eyes without a flinch.

My body caught in a seizure out of nowhere. The speed of my heartbeats fastened. Wetness covered my entire flesh. The sweat kept dropping rapidly on the floor. My eyes blurred, and all the things in the room disappeared from my vision, including faceless man.

The strangeness was gone; and all my senses returned. I opened my eyes, and the faceless man was still standing tall right in front of me like a statue. I looked around the room, and my gaze caught the transparent room. I couldn't believe my eyes—Ratanaporn. Her flesh lay on the bed naked, eyes closed, lying on side, knees up to her chest, like an unborn innocent baby in her mother's womb.

It pierced into my soul. The faceless man stabbed deep into my chest. His head got closer to my right ear.

"Verily, we forgive your sins. You are forgiven for committing adultery with girls. You are purified now. This is a rebirth moment for you. You are destined to get married to Ratanaporn. Do not commit pre-marital sex with her. Regardless of how much you love each other, be patient until you get married. Once you break your purification, committing pre-marital sex with her, you will face bad consequences. You will be doomed, cursed for the rest of your life." He conveyed his message to me, and took the knife out of my chest.

"My time is over. Our mission is done for you. Remember, Daler, we will be watching you. Remember!"

Sounds of the Waves

Unusually, the night sky looks crystal clear. All the stars, from the tiniest one to the largest, are visible to the eyes. The orange moon has shown in its full beautiful shape. The city is busy as usual, with cars roaming around and people in the streets. Here I am, taking Ratanaporn to Umm Suqeim beach. We are in a cab, sitting next to each other, holding our hands tightly. The cab has almost arrived at the destination.

As a promise to her, I decided to take her to that specific beach. She agreed to go at any time. We made up our minds to go after the sunset.

The weather cools down slightly, and the evening time is much more convenient. We left the apartment at 7:00 P.M., right after our dinner.

The cab arrives, and we are heading to the seashore to hear the **sounds of the waves.** While walking there, no words are coming out of our mouths as we are still holding hands.

We are on the seashore now. The breeze of the air makes the sounds of the waves more exotic.

"Look at the stars. There are so many of them tonight. Isn't it marvelous? I speak to her in a low, relaxing tone of voice, pointing."

"Yes, it is," she responds, clinging more to me.

I grab her waist, hugging her while both of us gaze at the stars. I am enjoying every bit of it right now. I am the happiest young man alive.

The orange moon is covering my gaze at the stars. I suddenly realize I am left all alone. Ratanaporn has vanished from my side. I cannot fathom what is happening now. I am kneeling down on my knees. I want to cry, but nothing is flowing from my cheeks. There is nobody around. Only the orange moon and I are here. I am trying to call, to scream for help, but to no avail.

My voice is gone; not a single word is making a noise. The pain is all over my body and in my soul. I can't, I can't endure.

I open my eyes, full of sweat. All alone, vague thoughts. "Ratanaporn, Ratanaporn," I call her name helplessly from my bed. She slips her hand under the blanket, grabs my left hand. I look at her side. "I am here, Daler, I am here," she says, looking into my eyes.